An Underground Walk

Ruskin Bond has been writing for over sixty years, and now has over 120 titles in print—novels, collections of short stories, poetry, essays, anthologies and books for children. His first novel, *The Room on the Roof*, received the prestigious John Llewellyn Rhys Prize in 1957. He has also received the Padma Shri (1999), the Padma Bhushan (2014) and two awards from Sahitya Akademi—one for his short stories and another for his writings for children. In 2012, the Delhi government gave him its Lifetime Achievement Award.

Born in 1934, Ruskin Bond grew up in Jamnagar, Shimla, New Delhi and Dehradun. Apart from three years in the UK, he has spent all his life in India, and now lives in Mussoorie with his adopted family.

An Underground Walk

Selected and Compiled by

RUSKIN BOND

RUPA

Published by Rupa Publications India Pvt. Ltd 2018
7/16, Ansari Road, Daryaganj
New Delhi 110002

Sales centres:
Allahabad Bengaluru Chennai
Hyderabad Jaipur Kathmandu
Kolkata Mumbai

ISBN: 978-93-5333-428-4

Third impression 2020

10 9 8 7 6 5 4 3

Printed at Saurabh Printers Pvt. Ltd, Noida

Contents

Introduction

I was sent to a boarding school in Shimla at a very young age. That old school though had a very eerie feel to it with its long corridors, unused rooms and thick forest right behind it. It encouraged my indulgence in the macabre. I spent hours of my free time sitting in the library and devouring all the tales of phantoms, ghosts, vampires and haunted houses that I could find. The ones I couldn't finish in the library were taken for reading at night under the bed covers with the help of a flashlight.

It was during that time that I discovered some masters of the genre such as R.L. Stevenson, Sylvia Green, Oscar Cook, John Eyton, C.A. Kincaid, Maurice Hewlett, and many others. In this book, I've collected some of the most blood-curdling tales penned by these writers with the hope that it will make for perfect company on a lonely winter night when you are warmly tucked in your bed.

As Thomas Ligotti once wrote, 'The sinister, the terrible never deceive: the state in which they leave us is always one of enlightenment. And only this condition of vicious insight allows us a full grasp of the world, all things considered, just as a frigid melancholy grants us full possession of ourselves. We may hide from horror only in the heart of horror.'

Ruskin Bond

THE MAN-EATER OF MUNDALI

B.B. Osmaston

Jaunsar-Bawai, which includes Chakrata, is an outlying portion of the Civil District of Dehra Dun. It is situated north-west of Dehra, between Mussoorie and Simla, and is very mountainous throughout, the hills ranging from 2,000 to 10,000 feet in altitude. These hills, except on southern aspects, are mostly clothed with forests of deodar, fir, pine, oak, etc., and mountain streams and torrents flow through the valleys. In summer, the climate is pleasantly cool, but very cold in winter, with heavy falls of snow down to 6,000 feet. There was much game in the form of gooral, barking deer, serow, musk deer and leopard; also partridges, chukor and several species of pheasants. Sambhar pig were scarce, and chiral, absent altogether. Tigers literally avoid these hill forests, not because they dislike the cold, but because they find feeding themselves difficult, if not impossible. In the plains sambhar and chiral constitute their main food supply, but these are scarce or non-existent in the hills.

Moreover, a tiger is unable to pursue and catch smaller game, such as gooral, which take refuge on steep slopes where a tiger, due to its weight, cannot safely follow. In 1878, however, a tigress suddenly appeared beyond Chakrata, at about 9,000 feet; she is believed to have come up from Dehra Dun, having followed the Gujars' buffaloes on their spring migration up to the hills.

These Gujars are a nomadic race of graziers, and own herds of magnificent buffaloes, which they maintain largely in the Government forests, feeding them mainly loppings from trees. During the winter months, they keep to the forests in the plains, but in April, they start driving their cattle up to the hills where they remain throughout the summer and rains, at altitudes between 7,000 and 11,000 feet; and in October, before the advent of snow, they take them down again.

But, to return to the tigress in question. Having followed the Gujars' cattle up to the hills, killing and feeding on stragglers from the herds during their 60–80 miles slow-moving trek, she their settled down to an easy and comfortable existence in the vicinity of the Gujars' camps, without any food problems whatever! But when October came, and the Gujars started driving their cattle down to the plains again, she seems to have either accidentally missed their departure, or, more likely, to have been more or less compelled to remain behind because she had meanwhile produced three babies which were still entirely dependent on her, and far too young to travel.

She thus, all at once, found herself and her cubs stranded, up at some 8,000 to 9,000 feet, with snow in the offing, and normal food supplies virtually non-existent. She and her farnil soon became desperately hungry and, one day while she was out hunting, she suddenly came across a man at close quarters, and, in her extremity, she killed him. She found that he was both ridiculously easy to kill, and also excellent to eat.

This led to her rapidly becoming a confirmed, notorious and cunning man-eater, taking toll from villages scattered over some 200 square miles of mountainous country. The villagers were terror-stricken and would not go out except in large parties. Even so, her killings continued, either by day or by night, and more often than not, it was a woman she selected.

She brought up her three cubs on human flesh and they too became man-eaters. They, however, lacked the cunning of their mother and were killed long before she was accounted for: one was killed by a spring-gun set by Mr Lowrie at Lokhar; another was shot near Chakrata by Mr Smythies, who obtained the assistance of British soldiers to surround the valley in which the young tiger had been located; the third cub was found dead under a tree which appeared to have been struck by lightning. The tigress, however, had continued in her evil ways, until in 1879 a reward of ₹500 was placed on her head. This had resulted in many visits from experienced shikaris, but none had ever succeeded in getting in touch with her, and the reward remained unclaimed for ten long years.

That was the picture when I arrived at Mundali on 11 May 1889. I had been in India less than five months and had never seen a tiger outside a zoo. The day I reached Mundali, I heard that the tigress had killed a buffalo calf, about half a mile from our camp. The latter included Forest Students from Dehra Dun, in the charge of Mr Fernandez, Deputy Director of the Forest School. I determined to tie up a machan in a tree near the kill, from which I hoped to get a shot at the tigress when she returned. But the same idea had also occurred to several of the students, and I foresaw little chance, therefore, of anyone at all getting a shot that way. However, a young fellow called Hansard, one of the students, approached me with a suggestion that we should explore the steep ravine below the kill at midday, when, we thought, the tigress would be enjoying a siesta. I readily agreed and we set out, I being armed with a double-barrelled twelve-bore rifle by Riley, firing a conical shell propelled by six drains of black powder, which was kindly lent by Mr Fernandez. Hansard had only a small bore rifle, which I later realized was quite inadequate for the purpose.

The kill was situated at the head of a precipitous ravine which had extremely steel-wooded sides, and a small spring stream at the bottom, bubbling down through a wild confusion of countless large and small boulders. It was under the lee of one of these large rocks that we were hoping, perhaps, to find the tigress asleep; and with that end in view, we cautiously started off down the ravine—I on one side fairly close to the stream, while Hansard was some 20 yards higher up on the other side.

The going was very difficult and slow, and we had not managed to get very far, when I suddenly heard a fierce snarling noise from moderately high up on the further side of the ravine. I momentarily imagined that it was Hansard trying to pull my leg; but, upon raising my head to tell him to shut up and keep quiet, I saw, to my horror, the tigress on top of him, biting at his neck.

It is extraordinary with what lightning speed thoughts can flash through one's brain in an emergency of that nature; and, in a matter of perhaps half a second, I knew that I must shoot—whatever the danger, of hitting Hansard, instead of or as well as the tigress—and in the next half second I had fired. The tigress immediately let go of Hansard and came charging down at me. I fired the second barrel as she came bounding down (but without effect), and then dropped the empty rifle and fled for my life down the precipitous ravine, leaping wildly from boulder to boulder in my head-long flight, and expecting every moment to get the tigress on top of me. But after I had covered some distance without either breaking my neck or being seized by the tigress, I realized that I was not being pursued after all; and I decided to cut straight back through the forest to the camp, in order to get another rifle, and help for Hansard.

Several of the students and their servants accompanied me back to the spot, bringing with them a camp-bed for use as a stretcher. Upon arrival there, we found Hansard lying unconscious by the stream, and the tigress lying dead a few yards away. It was my first shot that had actually killed her, the second one having merely grazed one of her fore-paws.

We afterwards ascertained from Hansard that he never knew that she was stalking him until she was on him, and he certainly never had a chance to fire his rifle. He was wearing a thick woollen muffler rolled up round his neck which doubtless did much to save him. In spite of this, however, the tigress had mauled him terribly, one hole penetrating from below his ear into his throat. Bits of the red muffler were adhering to the claws of the tigress when we found her in the water. She was old, though exactly how old it was impossible to say; but her canine teeth were worn right down almost to the gums and one, at least, was badly decayed. Otherwise she appeared to be in good health, and had a very good coat. Her length was 8 feet 6 inches.

Hansard and the tigress were at once carried to the camp where the former's wounds were attended to by the Assistant Surgeon attached to the school-camp, and two days later, he was carried miles across the hills to Mussoorie on a stretcher. There he remained in the Station Hospital for some months and, when he was eventually discharged, in reasonably good shape, he married his hospital nurse, and they went to Ceylon, where he had another forest appointment.

Some years later, I met his son, who said that his father had eventually died from the after-effects of that terrible encounter. The day after the tigress was brought into camp, the villagers flocked in from near and far to see the body of the dreaded beast which had carried off so many of their friends and relations during the past ten years.

Many of them cut off little bits of the tigress' flesh and hung them as charms round the necks of their children. The killing of the tigress was reported to the government and the reward of ₹500 was duly paid to me; this was shared with Hansard, who certainly deserved it at least as much as I did.

[More than a hundred years later, a notice-hoard at Mundali still marks the spot where Osmaston shot the man-eater—Ed.]

BECKWITH'S CASE

Maurice Hewlett

The facts were as follows. Mr Stephen Mortimer Beckwith was a young man living at Wilsford in the Amesbury district of Wiltshire. He was a clerk in the Wilts and Dorset Bank at Salisbury, was married and had one child. His age at the time of the experience here related was twenty-eight. His health was excellent.

On 30 November 1887, at about ten o'clock at night, he was returning home from Amesbury, where he had been spending the evening at a friend's house. The weather was mild, with a rain-bearing wind blowing in squalls from the south-west. It was three-quarter moon that night, and although the sky was frequently overcast, it was at no time dark. Mr Beckwith, who was riding a bicycle and accompanied by his Fox-terrier, Strap, states that he had no difficulty in seeing and avoiding the stones cast down at intervals by the road-menders; that flocks of sheep in the hollows were very visible, and that passing Wilsford House he saw a barn owl quite plainly and remarked its heavy, uneven flight.

A mile beyond Wilsford House, Strap, the dog, broke through the quickset hedge upon his right-hand side and ran yelping up the down, which rises sharply just there.

Mr Beckwith, who imagined that he was after a hare, whistled him in, presently calling him sharply, 'Strap, Strap, come out of it.' The dog took no notice, but ran directly to a clump of gorse and bramble halfway up the down, and stood there in the attitude of a pointer, with uplifted paw, watching the gorse intently, and whining. Mr Beckwith was by this time dismounted, observing the dog. He watched him for some minutes from the road. The moon was bright, the sky at the moment free from cloud.

He himself could see nothing in the gorse, though the dog was undoubtedly in a high state of excitement. It made frequent rushes forward, but stopped short of the object that it saw and trembled. It did not bark outright, but rather whimpered—'a curious, shuddering crying noise', says Mr Beckwith. Interested by the animal's persistent and singular behaviour, he now sought a gap in the hedge, went through on to the down and approached the clumped bushes. Strap was so much occupied that he barely noticed his master coming; it seemed as if he dared not take his eyes off for one second from what he saw in there.

Beckwith, standing behind the dog, looked into the gorse. From the distance at which he stood, still he could see nothing at all. His belief then was that there was either a tramp in a drunken sleep, possibly two tramps, or a hare caught in a wire, or possibly even a fox. Having no stick with him, he did not care, at first, to go any nearer, and contented himself with urging on the Terrier. This was not very courageous of him, as he admits, and was quite unsuccessful. No verbal excitations could draw Strap nearer to the furze-bush. Finally, the dog threw up his head, showed his master the white arcs of his eyes and fairly howled at the moon. At this dismal sound Mr Beckwith was himself alarmed. It was, as he describes it—though he is an

Englishman—'uncanny'. The time, he owns, the aspect of the night, loneliness of the spot (midway up the steep slope of a chalk down), the mysterious shroud of darkness upon shadowed and distant objects, and flood of white light upon the foreground—all these circumstances worked upon his imagination.

He was indeed for retreat; but here Strap was of a different mind. Nothing would excite him to advance, but nothing, either, could induce him to retire. Whatever he saw in the furze-bush Strap must continue to observe. In the face of this, Beckwith summoned up his courage, took it in both hands and went much nearer to the furze-bushes, much nearer, that is, than Strap the Terrier could bring himself to go. Then, he tells us, he did see a pair of bright eyes far in the thicket, which seemed to be fixed upon his, and by degrees also a pale and troubled face. Here, then, was neither fox nor drunken tramp, but some human creature, man, woman, or child, fully aware of him and of the dog.

Beckwith, who now had surer command of his feelings, spoke aloud, asking, 'What are you doing there? What's the matter?' He had no reply. He went one pace nearer, being still on his guard, and spoke again. 'I won't hurt you,' he said. 'Tell me what the matter is.' The eyes remained unwinkingly fixed upon his own. No movement of the features could be discerned. The face, as he could now make it out, was very small—'about as big as a big wax dolls,' he says, 'of a longish oval, very pale.' He adds, 'I could see its neck now, no thicker than my wrist; and where its clothes began, I couldn't see any arms, for a good reason. I found out afterwards that they had been bound behind its back. I should have said immediately, "That's a girl in there", if it had not been for one or two plain considerations. It had not the size of what we call a girl, nor the face of what we mean by a child. It was, in fact, neither fish, flesh, nor fowl.

Strap had known that from the beginning, and now I was of Strap's opinion myself.'

Advancing with care, a step at a time, Beckwith presently found himself within touching distance of the creature. He was now standing with furze half-way up his calves, right above it, stooping to look closely at it; and as he stooped and moved now this way, now that, to get a clearer view, so the crouching thing's eyes gazed up to meet his, and followed them about, as if safety lay only in that never-shifting, fixed regard. He had noticed, and states in his narrative, that Strap had seemed quite unable, in the same way, to take his eyes off the creature for a single second.

He could now see that, of whatever nature it might be, it was in form and features, most exactly a young woman. The features, for instance, were regular and fine. He remarks in particular upon the chin. All about its face, narrowing the oval of it, fell dark, glossy curtains of hair, very straight and glistening with wet. Its garment was cut in a plain circle round the neck and shorn off at the shoulders, leaving the arms entirely bare. This garment, shift, smock or gown, as he indifferently calls it, appeared thin, and was found afterwards to be of a grey colour, soft and clinging to the shape. It was made loose, however, and gathered in at the waist. He could not see the creature's legs, as they were tucked under her. Her arms, it has been related, were behind her back. The only other things to be remarked upon were the strange stillness of one who was plainly suffering, and might well be alarmed, an appearance of expectancy, a dumb appeal; what he himself calls rather well 'an ignorant sort of impatience, like that of a sick animal'.

'Come,' Beckwith now said, 'let me help you up. You will get cold if you sit here. Give me your hand, will you?' She neither spoke nor moved; simply continued to search his eyes. Strap, meantime, was still trembling and whining. But now, when he stooped yet lower to take her forcibly by the arms, she shrank back a little way and turned her head, and he saw to his horror that she had a great open wound in the side of her neck, from which, however, no blood was issuing. Yet it was clearly a fresh wound, recently made.

He was greatly shocked. 'Good God,' he said, 'there's been foul play here,' and whipped out his handkerchief. Kneeling, he wound it several times round her slender throat and knotted it as tightly as he could; then, without more ado, he took her up in his arms, under the knees and round the middle, and carried her down the slope to the road. He describes her as of no weight at all. He says it was 'exactly like carrying an armful of feathers about'. 'I took her down the hill and through the hedge at the bottom as if she had been a pillow.'

Here it was that he discovered that her wrists were bound together behind her back with a kind of plait of things so intricate that he was quite unable to release them. He felt his pockets for his knife, but could not find it, and then recollected suddenly that he should have a new one with him, the third prize in a whist tournament in which he had taken part that evening. He found it wrapped in paper in his overcoat pocket, with it cut the thongs and set the little creature free. She immediately responded—the first sign of animation which she had displayed by throwing both her arms about his body and clinging to him in an ecstasy. Holding him so that, as he says, he felt the shuddering go all through her, she suddenly lowered her head and touched his wrist with her cheek. He says that instead of being cold to the touch, 'like a fish', as she had seemed to be when he first took her out of the gorse, she was now 'as warm as toast, like a child'.

So far he had put her down for 'a foreigner', convenient term for defining something which one does not quite understand. She had none of his language, evidently; she was undersized, some, three feet six inches, by the look of her, and yet perfectly proportioned. She was most curiously dressed in a frock cut to the knee, and actually in nothing else at all. It left her barelegged and bare-armed, and was made, as he puts it himself, of stuff like cobweb, 'those dusty, drooping kind which you put on your finger to stop bleeding'. He could not recognize the web, but was sure that it was neither linen nor cotton. It seemed to stick to her body wherever it touched a prominent part. 'You could see very well, to say nothing of feeling, that she was well-made and well-nourished.' She ought, as he judged, to be a child of five years old, 'and a feather-weight at that'; but he felt certain that she must be 'much more like sixteen'. It was that, I gather, which made him suspect her of being something of an outside experience. So far, then, it was safe to call her a foreigner: but he was not yet at the end of his discoveries.

Heavy footsteps, coming from the direction of Wilsford, in due time proved to be of Police Constable Gulliver, a neighbour of Beckwith's and guardian of the peace in his own village. He lifted his lantern to flash it into the traveller's eyes, and dropped it again with a pleasant 'good evening'. He added that it was inclined to be showery, which was more than true, as it was, at the moment, raining hard. With that, it seems, he would have passed on.

But Beckwith, whether smitten by self-consciousness of having been seen with a young woman in his arms at a suspicious hour of the night by the village policeman, or bursting perhaps with the importance of his affair, detained Gulliver. 'Just look at this,' he said boldly. 'Here's a pretty thing to have found on a lonely road. Foul play somewhere, I'm afraid,' he then exhibited his burden to the lantern light.

To his extreme surprise, however, the constable, after exploring the beam of light and all that it contained for some time in silence, reached out his hand for the knife which Beckwith still held open. He looked at it on both sides, examined the handle and gave it back. 'Foul play, Mr Beckwith?' he said, laughing. 'Bless you, they use bigger tools than that. That's just a toy, the like of that. Cut your hand with it, though, already, I see.' He must have noticed the handkerchief, for as he spoke the light from his lantern shone full upon the face and neck of the child, or creature, in the young man's arms, so clearly that, looking down at it, Beckwith himself could see the clear grey of its intensely watchful eyes, and the very pupils of them, diminished to specks of black. It was now, therefore, plain to him that what he held was a foreigner indeed, since the parish constable was unable to see it. Strap had smelt it, then seen it, and he, Beckwith, had seen it; but it was invisible to Gulliver. 'I felt now,' he says in his narrative, 'that something was wrong. I did not like the idea of taking it into the house; but I intended to make one more trial before I made up my mind about that. I said good night to Gulliver, put her on my bicycle and pushed her home. But first of all I took the handkerchief from her neck and put it in my pocket. There was no blood upon it, that I could see.'

His wife, as he had expected, was waiting at the gate for him. She exclaimed, as he had expected, upon the lateness of the hour. Beckwith stood for a little in the roadway before the house, explaining that Strap had bolted up the hill and had had to be looked for and fetched back. While speaking he noticed that

Mrs Beckwith was as insensible to the creature on the bicycle as Gulliver the constable had been. Indeed, she went much farther to prove herself so than he, for she actually put her hand upon the handle-bar of the machine, and in order to that, drove it right through the centre of the girl crouching there. Beckwith saw that done. 'I declare solemnly upon my honour,' he writes, 'that it was as if Mary had drilled a hole clean through the middle of her back. Through gown and skin and bone and all her arm went; and how it went in I don't know. To me it seemed that her hand was on the handle-bar, while her upper arm, to the elbow, was in between the girl's shoulders. There was a gap from the elbow downwards where Mary's arm was inside the body; then from the creature's diaphragm her lower arm, wrist and hand came out. And all the time we were speaking the girl's eyes were on my face. I was now quite determined that I wouldn't have her in the house for a mint of money.'

He put her, finally, in the dog-kennel. Strap, as a favourite, lived in the house; but he kept a Greyhound in the garden, in a kennel surrounded by a sort of run made of iron poles and galvanized wire. It was roofed in with wire also, for the convenience of stretching a tarpaulin in wet weather. Here it was that he bestowed the strange being rescued from the down. It was clever, I think, of Beckwith to infer that what Strap had shown respect for would be respected by the Greyhound, and certainly bold of him to act upon his inference. However, events proved that he had been perfectly right. Bran, the Greyhound, was interested, highly interested, in his guest. The moment he saw his master, he saw what he was carrying. 'Quiet, Bran, quiet there,' was a very unnecessary adjuration. Bran stretched up his head and sniffed, but went no farther; and when Beckwith had placed his burden on the straw inside the kennel, Bran lay down, as if on guard, outside the opening and put his muzzle on his forepaws. Again Beckwith noticed that curious appearance of the eyes which the Fox-terrier's had made already. Bran's eyes were turned upwards to show the narrow arcs of white.

Before he went to bed, he tells us, but not before Mrs Beckwith had gone there, he took out a bowl of bread and milk to his patient. Bran, he found to be still stretched out before the entry; the girl was nestled down in the straw, as if asleep or prepared to be so, with her face upon her hand. Upon an afterthought he went back for a clean pocket handkerchief, warm water and a sponge. With these, by the light of a candle, he washed the wound, dipped the rag in hazeline and applied it. This done, he touched the creature's head, nodded a good night and retired. 'She smiled at me very prettily,' he says. 'That was the first time she did it.'

There was no blood on the handkerchief which he had removed.

Early in the morning, following upon the adventure, Beckwith was out and about. He wished to verify the overnight experiences in the light of refreshed intelligence. On approaching the kennel he saw at once that it had been no dream. There, in fact, was the creature of his discovery playing with Bran the Greyhound, circling sedately about him, weaving her arms, pointing her toes, arching her graceful neck, stooping to him, as if inviting him to sport, darting away—'like a fairy,' says Beckwith, 'at her magic, dancing in a ring.' Bran, he observed, made no effort to catch her, but crouched rather than sat, as if ready to spring. He followed her about with his eyes as far as he could; but when the course of her dance took her immediately behind him, he did not turn his head, but kept his eye fixed as far backward as he could, against the moment when she should come again into the scope of his vision. 'It seemed as important to him, as it had the day before to Strap, to keep her always in his eye. It seemed—and always seemed so long as I could study them together—intensely important.' Bran's mouth was stretched to 'a sort of grin'; occasionally he panted. When Beckwith entered the kennel and touched the dog (which took little notice of him), he found him trembling with excitement. His heart was heating at a great rate. He also drank quantities of water.

Beckwith, whose narrative, hitherto summarized, I may now quote, tells us that 'the creature was indescribably graceful and lightfooted. You couldn't hear the fall of her foot: you never could. Her dancing and circling about the cage seemed to be the most important business of her life; she was always at it, especially in bright weather. I shouldn't have called it restlessness so much as busyness. It really seemed to mean more to her than exercise or irritation at confinement. It was evident also that she was happy when so engaged. She used to sing. She sang also when she was sitting still with Bran; but not with such exhilaration.

'Her eyes were bright—when she was dancing about—with mischief and devilry. I cannot avoid that word, though it does not describe what I really mean. She looked wild and outlandish and full of fun, as if she knew that she was teasing the dog, and yet couldn't help herself. When you say of a child that he looks wicked, you don't mean it literally; it is rather a compliment than not. So it was with her and her wickedness. She did look wicked, there's no mistake—able and willing to do wickedness; but I am sure she never meant to hurt Bran. They were always firm friends, though the dog knew very well who was the master.

'When you looked at her you did not think of her height. She was so complete; as well-made as a statuette. I could have spanned her waist with my two thumbs and middle fingers, and her neck (very nearly) with one hand. She was pale and inclined to be dusky in complexion, but not so dark as a gypsy; she had grey eyes, and dark brown hair, which she could sit upon if she chose. Her gown you could have sworn was made of cobweb; I don't know how else to describe it. As I had suspected, she wore nothing else, for while I was there that first morning, so soon as the sun came up over the hill, she slipped it off her and stood dressed in nothing at all. She was a regular little Venus, that's all I can say. I never could get accustomed to that weakness of hers for slipping off her frock, though no doubt it was very absurd. She had no sort of shame in it, so why on earth should I?

'The food, I ought to mention, had disappeared: the bowl was empty. But I know now that Bran must have had it. So long as she remained in the kennel or about my place she never ate anything, nor drank either. If she had I must have known it, as I used to clean the run out every morning. I was always particular about that. I used to say that you couldn't keep dogs too clean. But I tried her unsuccessfully, with all sorts of things: flowers, honey, dew—for I had read somewhere that fairies drink dew and suck honey out of flowers. She used to look at the little messes I made for her, and when she knew me better, would grimace at them, and look up in my face and laugh at me.

'I have said that she used to sing sometimes. It was like nothing that I can describe. Perhaps the wind in the telegraph wires comes nearest to it, and yet that is an absurd comparison. I could never catch any words; indeed, I did not succeed in learning a single word of her language. I doubt very much whether they have what we call a language—I mean, the people who are like her, her own people. They communicate with each other, I fancy, as she did with my dogs, inarticulately, but with perfect communication and understanding on either side. When I began to teach her English, I noticed that she had a kind of pity for me, a kind of contempt perhaps is nearer the mark, that I should be compelled to express myself in so clumsy a way. I am no philosopher, but I imagine that our need of putting one word after another may be due to our habit of thinking in sequence. If there is no such thing as Time in the other world, it should not be necessary there to frame speech in sentences at all. I am sure that Thumbeline (which was my name for her; I never learned her real name) spoke with Bran and Strap in flashes, which revealed her whole thought at once. So also they answered her, there's no doubt. So also she contrived to talk with my little girl, who, although she was four years old and a great chatterbox, never attempted to say a single word of her own language to Thumbeline, yet communicated with her by the hour together. But I did not know anything of this for a month or more, though it must have begun almost at once.

'I blame myself for it, myself only. I ought, of course, to have remembered that children are more likely to see fairies than grownups; but then—why did Florrie keep it all a secret? Why did she not tell her mother, or me, that she had seen a fairy in Bran's kennel? The child was as open as the day, yet she concealed her knowledge from both of us without the least difficulty. She seemed the same careless, laughing child she had always been; one could not have supposed her to have a care in the world; and yet for nearly six months she must have been full of care, having daily secret intercourse with Thumbeline and keeping her eyes open all the time lest her mother or I should find her out. Certainly she could have taught me something in the way of keeping secrets. I know that I kept mine very badly, and blame myself more than enough for keeping it at all. God knows what we might have been spared, if, on the night I brought her home, I had told Mary the whole truth! And yet how could I have convinced her that she was impaling someone with her arm while her hand rested on the bar of the bicycle? Is not that an absurdity on the face of it? Yes, indeed; but the sequel is no absurdity. That's the terrible fact.

'I kept Thumbeline in the kennel for the whole winter. She seemed happy enough there with the dogs, and, of course, she had had Florrie, too, though I did not find that out until the spring. I don't doubt, now, that if I had kept her in there altogether, she would have been perfectly contented.

'The first time I saw Florrie with her, I was amazed. It was a Sunday morning. There was our four-year-old child standing at the wire, pressing herself against it, and Thumbeline close to her. Their faces almost touched; their fingers were interlaced; I am certain that they were speaking to each other in their own fashion, by flashes, without words. I watched them for a bit; I saw Bran come and sit up on his haunches and join them. He looked from one to another, and all about; and then he saw me.

'Now that is how I know that they were all three in communication, because, the very next moment, Florrie turned round and ran to me, and said in her pretty baby-talk, "Talking to Bran. Florrie talking to Bran." If this was willful deceit, it was most accomplished. It could not have been better done. "And who else were you talking to, Florrie?" I said. She fixed her round blue eyes upon me, and said shortly, "No-one else." And I could not get her to confess or admit, then or at any time afterwards, that she had any cognizance at all of the fairy in Bran's kennel, although their communications were daily, and often lasted for hours at a time. I don't know that it makes things any better, but I have thought sometimes that the child believed me to be as insensible to Thumbeline as her mother was. She can only have believed it at first, of course, but that may have prompted her to a concealment which she did not afterwards care to confess to.

'Be this as it may, Florrie, in fact, behaved with Thumbeline exactly as the two dogs did. She made no attempt to catch her at her circlings and wheelings about the kennel, nor to follow her wonderful dances, nor (in her presence) to imitate them. But she was (like the dogs) aware of nobody else when under the spell of Thumbeline's personality; and when she had got to know her, she seemed to care for nobody else at all. I ought, no doubt, to have foreseen that and guarded against it.

'Thumbeline was extremely attractive. I never saw such eyes as hers, such mysterious fascination. She was nearly always good-tempered, nearly always happy; but sometimes, she had fits of temper and kept herself to herself. Nothing then would get her out of the kennel, where she would lie curled up like an animal with her knees to her chin and one arm thrown over her face. Bran was always wretched at these times, and did all he knew to coax her out. He ceased to care for me or my wife after she came to us, and instead of being wild at the prospect of his Saturday and Sunday runs, it was hard to get him along. I had to take him on a lead until we had turned to go home; then he would set off by himself, in spite of hallooing and scolding, at a long steady gallop, and one would find him waiting crouched at the gate of his run, and Thumbeline on the ground inside it, with her legs crossed like tailor, mocking and teasing him with her wonderful shining eyes. Only once or twice did I see her worse than sick or sorry; then she was transported with rage and another person altogether. She never touched me—and why or how I had offended her I have no notion—but she buzzed and hovered about me like an angry bee. She appeared to have wings, which hummed in their furious movement; she was red in the face; her eyes burned; she grinned at me and ground her little teeth together. A curious shrill noise came from her, like the screaming of a gnat or hover-fly; but no words, never any words. Bran showed me his teeth too, and would not look at me. It was very odd.

'When I looked in, on my return home, she was as merry as usual, and as affectionate. I think she had no memory.

'I am trying to give all the particulars I was able to gather from my observation. In some things she was difficult, in others very easy to teach. For instance, I got her to learn in no time that she ought to wear her clothes, such as they were, when I was with her. She certainly preferred to go without them, especially in the sunshine; but by leaving her, the moment she slipped her frock off, I soon made her understand that if she wanted me she must behave herself according to my notions of behaviour. She got that fixed in her little head, but even so she used to do her best to hoodwink me. She would slip out one shoulder when she thought I wasn't looking, and before I knew where I was, half of her would be gleaming in the sun like satin. Directly I noticed it. I used to frown, and then she would pretend to be ashamed of herself, hang her head and wriggle her frock up to its place again. However, I could never teach her to keep her skirts about her knees. She was as innocent as a baby about that sort of thing.

'I taught her some English words, and a sentence or two. That was towards the end of her confinement to the kennel, about March. I used to touch parts of her, or of myself, or

Bran, and peg away at the names of them. Mouth, eyes, ears, hands, chest, tail, back, front: she learned all those and more. Eat, drink, laugh, cry, love, kiss, those also. As for kissing (apart from the word) she proved herself to be an expert. She kissed me, Florrie, Bran, Strap, indifferently, one as soon as another, and any rather than none, and all four for choice.

'I learned some things myself, more than a thing or two. I don't mind owning that one thing was to value my wife's steady and tried affection far above the wild love of this unbalanced, unearthly little creature, who seemed to be like nothing so much as a woman with the conscience left out. The conscience, we believe, is the still small voice of the Deity crying to us in the dark recesses of the body; pointing out the path of duty; teaching respect for the opinion of the world, for tradition, decency and order. It is thanks to conscience that a man is true and a woman modest. Not that Thumbeline could be called immodest, unless a baby can be so described or an animal. But could I be called true? I greatly fear that I could not—in fact, I know it too well. I meant no harm; I was greatly interested; and there was always before me the real difficulty of making Mary understand that something was in the kennel which she couldn't see. It would have led to great complications, even if I had persuaded her of the fact. No doubt she would have insisted on my getting rid of Thumbeline—but how on earth could I have done that if Thumbeline had not chosen to go? But, for all that, I know very well that I ought to have told her, cost what it might. If I had done it I should have spared myself lifelong regret, and should only have gone without a few weeks of extraordinary interest, which I now see clearly could not have been good for me, as not being founded upon any revealed Christian principle, and most certainly were not worth the price I had to pay for them.

'I learned one more curious fact which I must not forget. Nothing would induce Thumbeline to touch or pass over anything made of zinc. I don't know the reason for it; but gardeners will tell you that the way to keep a plant from slugs is to put a zinc collar round it. It is due to that I was able to keep her in Bran's run without difficulty. To have got out she would have had to pass zinc. The wire was all galvanized.

'She showed her dislike of it in numerous ways: one was her care to avoid touching the sides or tops of the enclosure when she was at her gambols. At such times, when she was at her wildest, she was all over the place, skipping high like a lamb, twisting like a leveret, wheeling round and round in circles like a young dog, or skimming, like a swallow on the wing, above ground. But she never made a mistake; she turned in a moment or flung herself backward if there was the least risk of contact. When Florrie used to converse with her from outside, in that curious silent way the two had, it would always be the child that put its hands through the wire, never Thumbeline. I once tried to put her against the roof when I was playing with her. She screamed like a shot hare and would not come out of the kennel all day. There was no doubt at all about her feelings for zinc. All other metals seemed indifferent to her.

'With the advent of spring weather, Thumbeline became not only more beautiful, but wilder, and exceedingly restless. She now coaxed me to let her out, and against my judgement, I did it; she had to be carried over the entry; for when I had set the gate wide open and pointed her the way into the garden, she squatted down in her usual attitude of attention, with her legs crossed, and watched me, waiting. I wanted to see how she would get through the hateful wire, so went away and hid myself, leaving her alone with Bran. I saw her creep to the entry and peer at the wire. What followed was curious. Bran came up wagging his tail and stood close to her, his side against her head; he looked down, inviting her to go out with him. Long looks passed between them, and then Bran stooped his head, she put her arms around his neck, twined her feet about his foreleg, and was carried out. Then she became a mad thing, now bird now moth; high and low, round and round, flashing about the place for all the world like a humming-bird moth, perfectly beautiful in her motions (whose ease always surprised me), and equally so in her colouring of soft grey and dusky-rose flesh. Bran grew a puppy again and whipped about after her in great circles round the meadow. But though he was famous at coursing, and has killed his hares single-handed, he was never once near Thumbeline. It was a curious sight and made me late for business.

'By degrees she got to be very bold, and taught me boldness too, and (I am ashamed to say) greater degrees of deceit. She came freely into the house and played with Florrie up and down stairs; she got on my knee at meal-times, or evenings when my wife and I were together. Fine tricks she played with me, I must own. She spilled my tea for me, broke cups and saucers, scattered my patience cards, caught poor Mary's knitting wool and rolled it about the room. The cunning little creature knew that I dared not scold her or make any kind of fuss. She used to beseech me for forgiveness occasionally when I looked very glum, and would touch my cheek to make me look at her imploring eyes, and keep me looking at her till I smiled. Then she would put her arms round my neck and pull herself up to my level and kiss me, and then nestle down in my arms and pretend to sleep. By and by, when my attention was called off her, she would pinch me, or tweak my necktie, and make me look again at her wicked eye peeping out from under my arm. 1 had to kiss her again, of course, and at last she might go to sleep in earnest. She seemed able to sleep at any hour or in any place, just like an animal.

'I had some difficulty in arranging for the night when once she had made herself free of the house. She saw no reason whatever for our being separated; but I circumvented her by nailing a strip of zinc all round the door; and I put one around Florrie's too. I pretended to my wife that it was to keep out draughts. Thumbeline was furious when she found out how she had been tricked. I think she never quite forgave me for it. Where she hid herself at night I am not sure. I think on the sitting-room sofa; but on mild mornings I used to find her outdoors, playing round Bran's kennel.

'Strap, our Fox-terrier, picked up some rat-poison towards the end of April and died in the night. Thumbeline's way of taking that was very curious. It shocked me a good deal. She had never been so friendly with him as with Bran, though certainly more at ease in his company than mine. The night before he died, I remembered that she and Bran and he had been having high games in the meadow, which had ended by their all lying down together in a heap, Thumbeline's head on Bran's flank, and her legs between his. Her arm had been round Strap's neck in a most loving way. They made quite a picture for a Royal Academician; "Tired of Play" or "The End of it Romp" I can fancy he would call it. Next morning, I found poor old Strap stiff and staring, and Thumbeline and Bran at their games just the same. She actually jumped over him and all about him as if he had been a lump of earth or stone. Just some such thing he was to her; she did not seem able to realize that there was the cold body of her friend. Bran just sniffed him over and left him, but Thumbeline showed no consciousness that he was there at all. I wondered, was this heartlessness of obliquity? But I have never found the answer to my question.

'Now I come to the tragical part of my story, and wish with all my heart that I could leave it out. But beyond the full confession I have made to my wife, the County Police and the newspapers, I feel that I should not shrink from any admission that may be called for of how much I have been to blame. In May, on the 13 of May, Thumbeline, Bran and our only child, Florrie, disappeared.

'It was a day, I remember well, of wonderful beauty. I had left all three of them together in the water meadow, little thinking of what was in store for us before many hours. Thumbeline had been crowning Florrie with a wreath of flowers. She had gathered cuckoo-pint and marsh marigolds and woven them together, far more deftly than any of us could have done, into a chaplet. I remember the curious winding, wandering air she had been singing (without any words, as usual) over her business, and how she touched each flower first with her lips, and then brushed it lightly across her bosom before she wove it in. She had kept her eyes on me as she did it, looking up from under her brows, as if to see whether I knew what she was about.

'I don't doubt now but that she was bewitching Florrie by this curious performance, which every flower had to undergo separately: but fool that I was, I thought nothing of it at the time, and bicycled off to Salisbury, leaving them there.

'At noon my poor wife came to me at the Bank, distracted with anxiety and fatigue. She had run most of the way, she gave me to understand. Her news was that Florrie and Bran could not be found anywhere. She said that she had gone to the gate of the meadow to call the child in, and, not seeing her, or getting any answer, she had gone down to the river at the bottom. Here she had found a few picked wild flowers but no other traces. There were no footprints in the mud, either of a child or a dog. Having spent the morning with some of the neighbours in a fruitless search, she had now come to me.

'My heart was like lead, and shame prevented me from telling her the truth, as I was sure it must be. But my own conviction of it clogged all my efforts. Of what avail could it be to inform the police or organize search-parties, knowing what I knew only too well? However, I did put Gulliver in communication with the head office in Sarum, and everything possible was done. We explored a circuit of six miles about Wilsford; every fold of the hills, every spinney, every hedgerow was thoroughly examined. But that first night of grief had broken down my shame: I told my wife the whole truth in the presence of the Reverend Richard Walsh, the congregational minister, and in spite of her absolute incredulity, and, I may add, scorn, next morning I repeated it to Chief Inspector Notcutt of Salisbury. Particulars got into the local papers by the following Saturday: and next, I had to face the ordeal of the *Daily Chronicle, Daily News, Daily Graphic, Star* and other London journals. Most of these newspapers sent representatives to lodge in the village, many of them with photographic cameras. All this hateful notoriety I had brought upon myself, and did my best to bear like the humble, contrite Christian, which I hope I may say I have become. We found no trace of our dear one, and never have to this day. Bran, too, had completely vanished. I have not cared to keep a dog since.

'Whether my dear wife ever believed my account, I cannot be sure. She has never reproached me for my wicked thoughtlessness, that's certain. Mr Walsh, our respected pastor, who has been so kind as to read this paper, told me more than once that he could hardly doubt it. The Salisbury police made no comments upon it one way or another. My colleagues at the Bank, out of respect for my grief and sincere repentance, treated me with a forbearance for which I can never be too grateful. I need not add that every word of this is absolutely true. I made notes of the most remarkable characteristics of the being I called Thumbeline at the time of remarking them, and those notes are still in my possession.'

PENDLEBURY'S TROPHY

John Eyton

I

Arthur St John Pendlebury—known to his intimates as 'Pen'—was the beau ideal of the cavalry subaltern, with plenty of friends, money and self-assurance. Before he had been in the country a year, India was at his feet; this is not to say that he had overstudied her languages or customs, but that he had sufficient means for fulfilling any of his aspirations, which were limited to picnics, polo ponies and shikar trophies. To the latter his first long leave was devoted. To one who has stalked the Highland stag under the eye of an experienced man, the stag of Kashmir seems easy game, and satisfaction was in Pendlebury's eye as he ran it over his pile of kit on Rawalpindi station: new portmanteau; new gun-cases, containing his twelve-bore, his Mannlicher Schonhauer, his Holland and Holland High Velocity; fieldglasses and telescope; kodak, for recording triumphs; new tent, fully equipped with every device for comfort and cooking altogether a capital outfit, pointing to an interesting addition to the Scotch heads in the hall at Pendlebury, for he could not fail to bag a Kashmiri stag or two in three weeks. To this sentiment Ali Baksh, his Mohammedan servant, agreed in perfect English...

'capital man, Ali Baksh—a real treasure.'

The drive from Rawalpindi to Srinagar was quite pleasant, the scenery being almost English, though the road was only so-so. On arrival, Pendlebury resisted the tame temptations of picnic-making, and got down to business at once. He was not going to be bothered with consulting the old local bores in the Club, because the obvious thing to do was to get hold of a native fellow who could talk English a bit, and knew the ropes from A to Z, and such a man was known to Ali Baksh, who would find him out quietly and persuade him to accompany the saheb. His friend, he said, was the best man in Kashmir, who being in constant request, would accompany only noted shikaris. Ali Baksh tactfully insinuated that Pendlebury belonged to the latter category, and Pendlebury of course believed him—for even the finished product of Eton and the Bullingdon is often singularly artless in the experienced hands of an Indian bearer.

At eleven o'clock on the morning after arrival, Ali Baksh produced the paragon, whose name was also something Baksh Pir, Baksh, Pendlebury believed him to say. He was a fine-looking, well-set-up fellow, with fierce moustaches and glittering eyes; nicely turned out too, with a khaki suit of military cut, mauve shirt and neat puttees; he carried a long mountaineering pole, and had glasses slung in a leather case over his shoulder, and was altogether the type of what a shikari ought to look, and indeed does look in magazine illustrations. To the experienced old bores in the Club, he might have appeared to overdo the part, but to Pendlebury he was the very thing. Besides, he knew all the likely spots, had excellent chits from officers in quite good regiments, indicating invariable success, and, lastly, got on well with Ali Baksh.

So Pir Baksh was engaged on the spot—for the modest sum

of one hundred rupees, paid in advance, for the three weeks' trip, and on the understanding that he would waste no time over uncertainties, but would lead on direct to the spot where an astounding stag had been marked down. About this stag there was no doubt whatever, for Pir Baksh himself resided in its neighbourhood, and knew its haunts and habits so well that the stag might almost be said to be one of the family. He had been keeping it, he said, for a General, but could not resist the temptation of seeing it fall to the rifle of so noble a saheb as Pendlebury. They parted quite effusively, after payment had been made, and Ali Baksh accompanied Pir Baksh to make the bandobast. Pendlebury washed his hands of these matters, so naturally did not see Pir hand over the stipulated thirty rupees to his friend Ali outside.

As Pendlebury remarked in the mess on his return from leave. 'What I like about this country is that you only have to get hold of a good servant, tell him what you want to do and how you like it, and say *Bazar chalo, bandobast karo*. He'll do the rest. Now I had a first-class bandobast up in Kashmir—never had to say a word myself; no use messing a good man about.'

And so it was—his two men certainly were not messed about, for between them they did everything, and ran Pendlebury—engaging ponies and carriers on the basis of a twenty per cent commission for themselves; leading in men from the shops, who staggered beneath a vast weight of stores, some of which were destined for Pendlebury's consumption; making a great show of polishing things and cleaning clean rifles. There was nothing wrong with that bandobast, and Pendlebury could well afford to pay the hundred and fifty odd rupees, which it was found necessary to disburse. In fact, the charm of the whole thing was that Pendlebury believed throughout that he was saving money—a fact which redounds to the credit of the astute pair.

The start for the first camp was worth watching; first rode Pendlebury, every inch a cavalry officer, his blue eyes full of good humour, and his cheeks quite pink with excitement; his shooting suit was good to look upon, and Ali Baksh could certainly polish boots. At a respectful distance behind him rode Pir Baksh, resplendent in Jodhpur breeches, while, last of all, Ali marshalled the kit, a fine staff in one hand, and in the other that emblem of the bearer, a brass hurricane lamp. It was a procession to be proud of, and successful shikar was in the very air.

The haunt of the famous stage was ten marches away, and Pendlebury beguiled them with small-game shooting and the taking of snapshots. The marches were very well run, and it was not the fault of Pir Baksh that the leather suitcase, the telescope, and the cartridge bag got lost in the process of crossing a river. In fact, Pendlebury thought Pir Baksh had behaved very openly about the whole thing, and had seemed to regard the matter as a personal loss—whereas, in truth, it was exactly the opposite. But for this mishap all went swimmingly.

They reached the little village at the edge of the forest in the evening, and Pendlebury's tent was pitched under delightful chenal trees near a little stream which looked first-class for trout. He could hardly sleep for excitement, and lay awake picturing the record stag and its record head, and hearing the sound of a high-pitched song in the bazaar, where, had he but known it, Pir and Ali were entertaining the local shikaris at his expense. Finally, he shouted, '*Choop. Choop karo ek dam!*' and lay back with the satisfaction of one whose commands are obeyed.

Next day, it was arranged that Pir Baksh should go for khabar of the stag, while Pendlebury fished the river for trout.

So, Pendlebury sallied out with his split-cane and fly-boxes, and a man to carry his net, and another man to bear his lunch, while Pir Baksh, with his glasses and pole and preposterous jodhpuris, departed in the opposite direction. It was curious that so confident and so famous a shikari should require the assistance of a local man, a stranger of ragged and unkempt appearance—but we will suppose that he too needed some one to carry his lunch.

Pendlebury had a pleasant enough day by the bright, clear stream, and brought home several minute trout for his dinner. Of the movements of Pir Baksh little is known, except that he went quite a distance into the forest, starting at 10 a.m. and returning at noon, after which hour he sat with Ali and the local talent in the bazaar. Yet, when he was announced at 8 p.m., he entered the tent wearily enough, with much bazaar dust on his boots and puttees—so much that Pendlebury could see that the fellow had had a pretty stiff day of it. Pir Baksh was mysterious and confidential; in response to Pendlebury's eager inquiries, he allowed that he had seen the stag, but when Pendlebury whooped with delight, he qualified this intelligence with the remark that the stag was bahut hoshiar, and had only arrived on the scene in the late evening, after a complete day of tireless, lonely watching on the part of Pir Baksh. He had heard the stag at intervals and had not dared to move for fear of making it nervous. It would be as well to let it rest, under due observation, for a day or two, and then make certain of it. Incidentally, he had heard in the bazaar on his return that another saheb, a well-known hunter, had set his heart on this stag and had hunted it for a month, but, since he had not seen fit to engage the services of Pir Baksh, he had not had a shot. It was finally suggested that Pendlebury would do well to visit a noted pool three miles down stream for the next day or two, and this Pendlebury agreed to do. After all, Pir Baksh knew the ropes, and this stag was worth waiting for.

So for the next two days, Pendlebury lashed the stream for trout, while each morning Pir Baksh started with a set face for the jungle and spent the day in the bazaar, arriving each evening at a later hour and more visibly weary and dusty. Each evening, too, the antlers of the stag had grown with its cunning. Rowland Ward's book, which Pendlebury, of course, carried, had no record in it to touch this head, as described by Pir Baksh; to Rowland Ward the head should go for setting up—none of your local mochis. Pendlebury saw the footnote in that book, 'Shot by A. St J. Pendlebury, Esq, the Blue Hussars, Kashmir, 1920. A remarkable head, with record points, length and span'. On the third evening, Pir Baksh was very late indeed. Pendlebury had turned in, and had long lain listening to a perfect orgy in the bazaar, when, about midnight, Ali Baksh gave that deprecating cough whereby the Indian servant makes known his humble presence, and announced Pir Baksh.

A tired, grimy, dusty picture he made in the light of the electric torch, and a pitiful tale he told. He had sat up without food for a day and half a night

'Bahut kaam kiya, saheb. Main bilkull bhuka ho gya—bilkull. Kuchh nahin khaya gya.'

Great indeed had been the sufferings of the worthy man (considering they had been experienced in the bazaar), but he had seen the stag at close quarters, and something told him that the saheb would shoot it tomorrow.

Such a stag—a Barasingha indeed, with antlers like trees, and its roar like a river; such a stag had not been seen for twenty years, when 'Ismith' saheb had missed just such a one, and had given him, Pir Baksh, his new rifle and a hundred golis, vowing he would never shoot again...'*Kabhi ham aisa barawala nahin dekha.*' Pendlebury was, of course, half out of his mind with excitement, and, had it been feasible, he would have gone out there and then and tried conclusions. As it was, he contented himself with lauding Pir Baksh to the skies, an honour which the latter accepted with sweet humility. He would make the bandobast; they would start out after tiffin, and would lie up till the evening. Let the saheb have no doubts; he would slay that stag, and his name would be great in Kashmir...'*Kuchh shaqq nahin hai; qaza zarur hoga...zarur.*'

Like an echo outside the tent, Ali Baksh repeated the comforting 'zarur'.

II

Pendlebury arose at 6 a.m. for the stag which he was to see at 6 p.m., and spent the most nerve-racking morning of his life. He cut himself shaving; he fiddled with his rifles, and asked a dozen times whether he should take the High Velocity or the little Mannlicher; he counted out ten rounds of ammunition and laid them ready...then, decided to rake the other rifle, and counted out twenty more; then, finally changed his mind and decided to take both, with about thirty rounds; he stuffed his pipe too full, and broke the vulcanite stem in tapping it out; changed his boots three times; smoked quantities of cigarettes, and burnt a hole in his copy of Rowland Ward with one of them; and had neither a good breakfast nor a sufficient lunch.

In fact, Pendlebury did his utmost to spoil his eye and his hand, instead of strolling out with a rod and forgetting the great stag in the excitement of landing a pound trout, as any of the old bores at the Club would have advised him to do.

At last, the great moment arrived, and Ali Baksh whispered, 'Pir Baksh here, sir.' With an immense effort Pendlebury assumed the nonchalance he did not feel, and strolled out of the tent, where he found Pir Baksh carrying a rifle and looking very businesslike in ancient garments; a ragged, disreputable stranger had the other rifle. When Pendlebury, who was feeling nervous enough already, objected to the latter's presence, Pir Baksh pointed out the advantages of having a man on the spot to help skin the shikar, and so had his way. On the way, Pendlebury did a great many things which the old bores at the Club would have deprecated: he smoked too many cigarettes—'to steady his nerves'; he slogged along instead of walking quietly, thus laying up a clammy shirt for himself in the evening; also, he cursed the men for not hurrying, and then cursed still more when, halfway, he discovered that he had forgotten his second-best pipe, his flask and his sandwiches. However, it was too late to do anything then.

They climbed uphill through thick forest bordering a little hill stream till they came to an open glen, with green moss at their feet and tall trees around them. Halfway up the glen, Pir Baksh whispered a halt, and Pendlebury was led behind the trunk of a fallen tree, where he was asked to wait, without moving, while Pir Baksh and the stranger moved furtively off under the cover of the trees.

Hours seemed to pass as Pendlebury fingered his Mannlicher, the final choice, expecting every moment to see the dark shape loom in the glen. Time and time again, he opened his breech to see if the thing were working, and feverishly moved the backsight up and down the slide, finally, leaving it at five hundred yards, when a sudden sound startled him.

It was booming, long-drawn...the unmistakable roar of a

stag far above him. He was at once certain that Pir Baksh had messed up the whole show, and that he ought to be farther up the glen; it would be dark for a certainty before the stag moved down; it was getting dark already. A twig cracked behind him, and he turned to see Pir Baksh behind him, holding his finger to his lips.

'*Barawala ata*,' whispered Pir Baksh, while Pendlebury got into a position of readiness; there was no doubt about the approach of the stag, for it roared more than once, and was evidently moving down the little stream.

A quarter of an hour passed—the sun sank—still no view of the stag; in five minutes it would be too dark to see the foresight. Pendlebury began to fidget, when suddenly Pir Baksh touched his arm, and pointed…a dark shape was moving under the trees by the stream.

'*Woh hai, saheb*,' whispered Pir Baksh. '*Maro. Maro. Zarur lag jaega.*'

Pendlebury aimed his wavering piece in the direction of the dark shape, and squeezed the trigger…

There was a flash and a kick—then a commotion under the trees, as a big animal splashed with a snort through the tiny stream and crashed into the undergrowth beyond—farther and farther away.

'Damn!' said Pendlebury—not so Pir Baksh, who sprang to his feet with a wild, '*Lag gya. Lag gya. Zakhmi hai*,' and, motioning to Pendlebury to stay where he was, ran towards the stream, throwing out a parting, '*Milega zarur.*'

It was quite dark when Pir Baksh returned and informed the ecstatic Pendlebury that the stag '*sekht zakhmi ho gya. Khun bahut hai. Aiye, saheb.*' Up jumped Pendlebury and followed across the glen and the stream, where Pir Baksh borrowed his electric torch and searched the ground…yes, there was blood…first, a mere drop on a leaf; then, five yards on, a bigger splash; farther still, a regular patch dyeing the ground. Pir Baksh explained that the beast had been hit forward—a truly wonderful shot—and had carried on to die. He would be found quite dead in the morning—till then there was nothing to be done.

On the way home, Pir Baksh, in the intervals of exultation, promised to make an early start, dissuading Pendlebury from accompanying him by remarking that this was only poor shikari's work, unsuitable for the saheb bahadur. Pendlebury was fagged out, and let him have his way; before he went to bed, he had a last loving look at the Mannlicher, which he found sighted at five hundred yards! This he put down to carelessness in carrying, and congratulated himself that he had not had it at five hundred when he fired; good shot as it had been, he would not have put the beast at over seventy yards…funny how he had felt certain that he had hit him before Pir Baksh spoke!

III

Pendlebury's next morning was almost as bad as the last. He clung to the camp, springing out of his chair at the slightest sound; he had occasion to throw his boots at Ali because the latter had made a noise like Pir; once more, he failed to do justice to his meals, and spent the day alternating between triumph and despair. But the hours never brought Pir Baksh, and at last, he turned into bed and lay awake, listening. Presently, he heard a hubbub, then saw lights outside. As he sprang out of bed, he was greeted with the welcome, 'Mil gya…saheb,' in the dulcet tones of Pir Baksh; he rushed out, and there, amid a crowd of admiring servants, stood Pir Baksh himself, grimed with mud and dust from head to foot, his clothes artistically torn, blood on his coat but in his hands great antlers, branching out from a draggled mask.

Pendlebury whooped; the servants sucked in their breath with wonder; and Pir Baksh, in shrill tones, raised his paean of victory. Twenty miles had he toiled; fifteen hours without food; but for the saheb's honour he would have dropped with fatigue and died. Even in death, the great stag had been wondrous cunning, and would never have been brought to book but for the superior cunning of Pir Baksh; there had been a personal encounter, in which danger had been gladly braved for the saheb, and a valuable life risked. Great was the name of 'Pendlebury saheb', who gives life to poor men, even to the humble shikari, beneath his feet...

This stirring recital—composed that day in the bazaar—was followed by that little lull which tactfully indicates baksheesh to the least imaginative of us, and Pendlebury rose to the occasion nobly. There was a hundred-rupee note for Pir Baksh; twenty for the disreputable stranger who had given *bahri madad*, and who was described as a '*sidha admi...kam kerne wala bhi*'; twenty more for Ali Baksh for being a good fellow; and mithai for all the camp. Pendlebury did things handsomely.

▪

The old Club bores might, with reason, have sniffed at that head had they seen it; but, as it happens, it was packed straight off to Pendlebury's agents in Bombay, for shipping to London, on the advice of Pir Baksh—so there was no one to call attention to a resemblance between these antlers and a pair produced by the disreputable stranger aforesaid on the occasion of Pir Baksh's first visit to the bazaar. In point of fact, both pairs had a similar chip off of one of the brow points.

The stranger had asked twenty rupees for this pair...but who can fathom the mind of the East?

Another trivial detail...Pir Baksh and the said stranger had slain a young stag on the second day; while Pendlebury was fishing, for they had feasted the village with fresh venison that night. It was also on record that Pir Baksh had retained the mask, and had bottled a small quantity of blood.

One more fact—Pendlebury had been mistaken about his sighting, and the stag at which he fired in the dusk was not a warrantable one; at least, so the stranger informed me afterwards. Not that it matters, for the shot went well over its back.

But what matters? The great head has the pride of place at Pendlebury Hall, and Pendlebury is happy whenever he sees it.

And, anyway, Pir Baksh was an artist.

THE GREAT RETREAT

Aubrey Wade

The twenty-first of March 1918 is a date that can never be forgotten in the history of the Great War. It nearly spelled defeat for the Allies—it was the day that the great retreat began. This is the vivid story of a man who was with the artillery, and whose guns helped to cover that retreat. When the retreat began, they were stationed at Jussy, and it is at Jussy that his story opens.

At half-past four in the morning, I thought the world was coming to an end.

We awoke to the sound of debris, which was flying right and left from the explosion of a great shell somewhere near at hand. Before I had properly grasped what had occurred, another shell came down with a terrific roar just outside. I had a momentary glimpse of the end of the structure collapsing like a piece of stage scenery; the whole place shook about our ears with the violence of the explosion; I felt sure the next one would annihilate us. Frantically, I dragged on my clothes and cursed myself for being such a fool as to undress in spite of the warning. Shells were falling everywhere now in a heavy bombardment. More frequent flashes lit up the windows, and while I tugged desperately at my big field-boots, something ripped through the woodwork near my face. A great hole showed where it passed through the wall; my candle had disappeared, leaving me to scramble for the rest of my equipment in a darkness charged with terror.

And then, amid the crash of the shells, we heard a voice: 'Stand to the horses! Stand to the horses!'

There was a movement to the door, a careful hesitating advance into the darkness outside; one by one the drivers filed out and went over to the horse-lines on the other side of the field. I was last through the door, and on my way out, I spotted some one huddled up in bed right by the entrance. I knew whose bed it was, it was that of a certain lanky Scottish recruit, who was on the sick-list with boils all over him. I shook him urgently. 'Come on, man; you'll be killed if you stop here!'

A weak voice answered me from beneath the blankets: 'Och awa' wi' ye. I'm aff duty!'

'You'd better come. It's not safe here, mind.'

'I'm of duty, I tell ye!'

There was not much time to waste on a lunatic like that, so I gave him up and followed the others; and halfway over to the horses I was glad I had not waited any longer, for a shell shrieked into the exact centre of the four huts and must have killed him as he lay there.

In the stables, I took hold of my horse and led her out across the field to where the rest of the waggon-line occupants loomed up in the heavy fog that shrouded everything. It was a thick, cold, clammy sort of mist, so dense that it was impossible to see more than a few yards in front of one's face. Here, away from the huts, there were no shells dangerously close; the violence of the bombardment was concentrated on the huts, the village behind, and the roads to the line and back to Flavy. I stood with the reins looped over my arm, my little mare grazing quietly, for perhaps a quarter of an hour, getting a glimpse of the others now and then through the fog. A full hour passed, during which time the shelling seemed to get even worse, so that when I heard some one calling me by name, I guessed there had been something happening at the guns.

And I was not wrong. I was wanted to replace casualties.

Our little party of gunners and signallers left the waggonline as the mist was clearing. We could see the road quite plainly in front of us—so plainly, in fact, that we saw things on it which decided us not to take the road at all, but make a detour across country. Only a few hours previously, I had ridden along that road in the light of the stars, and it had seemed like a country road at home in its untouched whiteness; but now, it was different. The shells had torn great holes in its length, and with the shells had come the red splashes of death where ammunition-waggons and infantry transport had been caught in the open when the barrage started. Smashed vehicles festooned its borders; horses lay there rigid alongside them, and occasionally a blotch of khaki.

The gun-position looked somehow different. Something had been happening there, too. Shell-holes were dotted about between the guns, gaping holes which showed up glaringly against the smooth green of the turf, and the guns were in action with the covers off and piles of ammunition ready at the trails. No shells came over as we walked on to the position, and ahead in the line the landscape was beginning to show its accustomed outlines as the fog lifted. Outside the TDO, there was a little crowd of gunners, and an officer bending over someone who was lying on the grass at their feet. It was poor old Corporal S, of the signallers, who had caught it badly, and was about to be carried away to the dressing-station. I looked at his face as the stretcher passed me, and recognition came into his eyes. And then, they called me into the dugout to take over the telephone.

All the morning, the gunners 'stood' ready to fire as soon as we should hear where the enemy had got to in their advance. No information had come down yet except the tales the wounded had to tell of how they had been suddenly overwhelmed in the frontline and surrounded by hordes of Jerries in the fog. The enemy had broken through all right after the terrific bombardment of the early hours, but he was held up somewhere or other, and now and again, the rattle of machine guns came back to us.

The front grew quieter as the morning wore on. Shelling became less frequent. But the fog had cleared completely, and every moment we expected orders for action, now that observation of the enemy movements was possible. Towards midday, the noises of firing dropped to an occasional shell or so, and then, came silence. It was all very mysterious and alarming. What was happening up there in front? Should we see the Boches coming over?

It was half-past twelve when the first message came over the phone. Five minutes later, the range had been worked out and the battery was in action, banging away at some unseen target over the low slopes in front of us, wooded slopes towards which we had directed half-fearful glances during the morning. With minor alterations of range, the guns kept it up for the next hour, two rounds per gun per minute, and I seized the opportunity of getting out on the position to have a look at things.

Directly ahead the rising ground precluded all view of the line, so my sightseeing was limited to the flanks. On the right there was another battery in action about half a mile away, going strong with flashing salvoes. I looked to the left, and then I saw something which made my heart contract and sent me running back to the TDO to fetch Ross out to have a look.

The infantry was running away.

Down the slopes they came, throwing away their rifles as they ran, coming down towards the guns at the double in twos and threes, hatless and wholly demoralized, calling out to us as they passed that Jerry was through and that it was all over. No use staying there with those guns, they yelled as they ran by; he was through! Privates, non-commissioned officers, running for their lives out of the horror they had tried to stand up to all that day, running past our guns in increasing numbers, and making us realize to the full the desperate plight we were in. Why should we not retire as well and save the guns?

But the Major was out on the position now, tight-lipped and grim, swinging his revolver in his hand and telling us all that no man was to leave the guns without orders or he would be shot; watching the rise ahead and then glancing back at the broken remnant of the battalion fleeing in disorder; sweeping the skyline with his glasses for the first signs of grey figures coming over—we were to stay.

Towards three o'clock more and more infantry retired on our left and made us feel that we would shortly be the only people in the line at all. Messages came through with increasing rapidity ordering us to fire here and there on the advancing enemy. The ammunition was running out and an orderly was sent galloping off to the waggon-line for more. The whole brigade was now firing salvo after salvo into Lambay Wood, just in front, where masses of the Jerries were. Across the front, as far as the eye could see, there was no other artillery brigade firing; the one on our right had packed up at midday, and we were alone on the sector with the whole might of the enemy closing on us.

No more infantry came down now. There were no more there. Inquisitive aeroplanes had found the coast all clear for a general advance. Only our brigade held the line, firing desultory salvoes into Lambay Wood, sweeping the guns across a too-wide arc of the front in a futile attempt to stay the tide of field-grey that was spreading towards us out there in the darkness of the evening. Across the length and breadth of the sector, save only where our battery defiantly banged away and reloaded and banged again, there settled a prolonged silence. A faint and strangely alarming rumble of transport reached us at intervals from afar, as if the enemy had penetrated behind us on the flanks and was dragging up his artillery. We did not know. The hours went by to seven o'clock and then eight o'clock with still no order to retire. With the coming of night, the guns ceased their work, as the location of the enemy was now shrouded in mystery. The next thing that would happen, I thought, would be our last shoot of the war, at point-blank range, as they came running down that same slope with their bombs and bayonets.

It was long past nine o'clock when the jingling gun-teams broke from the gloom behind the position and bore down upon us urgently. In a flurry of excitement at our release, we hooked them in, working like mad at the swingle-trees of the limbers, grabbing telephones and equipment and running over our horses as soon as the guns were ready to pull out. I got mounted, looked around for Ross—ah, here he was, all aboard. The first of the guns was moving across the field now, and one by one the others dropped into line. We trotted ahead to our places. In a few minutes, the whole battery was safely out on the road and headed in the direction of Jussy, moving along at a fast walk that for me, at least, was not fast enough. My strained ears had detected, in the last few moments on the position, a nearer rumbling than ever of unseen transport, a murmuring of vast columns on the move through the night.

We retired through Jussy, taking a last look at the old familiar scenes of the waggon-line as we rode past, at the huts, now wrecked by the storm of shell-fire of that morning, at the low horse-shelters behind them; and presently we were riding through the next village of Flavy-le-Martel.

Here on the outskirts of the place the Major turned his horse off the main road and steered left in a southerly direction. Ahead of us, we could dimly make out the outline of a hill against the night sky, and we felt ourselves climbing a steady rise leading up to the summit of the hill, where we halted. Now, we were on a sort of plateau, from which we could look down on the almost-side-by-side villages of Jussy and Flavy. It was nearly midnight. We had travelled a good way back and felt much safer up there by Faillouel on the hill. I began to think about getting some sleep now that we were clear of immediate danger, but stood around for a while to find out what the orders were. There were no buildings near where we could billet; the guns had been run into position behind a low ridge in the open field so that if we slept at all, it would be under the sky with all our clothes on. Then the order was passed round that we were staying there for the night. I found there was nothing for the signallers to do, so I spread my waterproof sheet under a waggon, wrapped myself in my shell-shocked coat and a blanket, and slept. I and the rest of the battery slept for five hours. I mention this because it was the longest sleep we had for ten days and nights following this first stand at Faillouel.

It was cold up there on that plateau. Very early in the morning I awoke half frozen and scrounged two more blankets that some one had left lying about. The guard was pacing back and fore in rear of the silent guns. Another hour or so passed before morning dragged us all out to see how the war was going on down in the valley, and the smell of breakfast was in the air. Evidently there was no danger just yet. No firing had been done during the night, but the guns were ready for any eventuality with a round in the breech.

Quite a number of gunners, I noticed, were furtively eating biscuits and small cakes, and one or two of the more gluttonous were spreading the biscuits with condensed milk. Cigarettes were also in evidence, large packets of twenties and fifties that I stared at enviously, at the same time reflecting how foolish I had been not to have remembered that canteen in Flavy. The parsons had of course left everything they could not carry with them for the especial benefit of the troops following after; I determined to be on the lookout for the next canteen. We opened fire on the approaching German infantry at ten o'clock that morning.

During the day we got shelled intermittently from the direction of Montescourt, doubtless in response to messages sent back by the scouting aeroplane which cruised cheekily over Faillouel and the battery, with no opposition from antiaircraft guns. Nothing came near enough to do any damage, however. All day the guns flashed and cracked from the plateau with a steadily decreasing range as the Fritzes came on through Jassy in the valley below us. The rate of advance was slower now. Evidently they were chary of penetrating farther into open country where our task of dropping high-explosive into them would be ever so much easier, preferring to hold on until their artillery could be brought to bear on the brigade that incessantly spoilt their crossing of the canal. A rumour spread that cavalry had been seen behind Jussy.

The short March afternoon waned, twilight fell, and still the guns kept up their barrage. Night found them lighting up the scrubby plateau with the six-fold flash of salvoes interspersed with successive rounds of gun-fire; no rest for the gunners and no friendly rolling of supporting artillery on either flank such as we were wont to hear in the line. In the small hours firing ceased for a while; then as soon as it was daylight somehow other information came through, which woke the guns again.

At midday there was more shelling and this time with more accuracy of aim, which was not to be wondered at now that they could look straight up at the battery-smoke on our plateau. Some of us scattered out of the way right over to the end of the field from where we found it was possible to see a wide stretch of what lay in front; and by dint of keeping careful watch I saw for the first time real live Germans on the warpath against us. They were a good way off, but the helmets were unmistakable.

Towards one o'clock came the disheartening sight of small detachments of our own infantry retiring on both sides of us. They came back in little knots of twos and threes, scattered wide apart. Seeing them made us more anxious than ever to get out to the crossroads before our way of escape was quite cut off. But right up to the last we were kept at it, firing now with the gun-teams hooked in alongside and the whole battery in a growing state of anticipation. From the smoke-covered position itself the actual front could not be seen, the banks of the lane obstructing our view, and our consequent ignorance . of the movements of the enemy added to our alarm.

Then all of a sudden the gun stopped firing. I looked

round. A messenger was galloping off to the other batteries, his horse's hoofs strumming across the plateau. There was a yell of 'Limber up!', and in a moment the guns were hidden by the swift-wheeling teams manoeuvring for the hook-in. Sharp orders rattled out. The position was now a confusion of horses, guns and men, a confusion that straightened itself out as the first team drew clear and made for the gate. I leapt into the saddle, beckoned to Ross, and struck off after them before the next team should come through and perhaps get stuck in the difficult gateway. The first gun had managed it all right and was out in the lane waiting for the others, perhaps two hundred yards away from the gate. We rode to the head of them, dismounted for fear of observation up there on horseback, and hung about consumed with impatience at the time the rest of the battery were taking to follow us. At painfully slow intervals the teams struggled through and joined the column. Now there remained only one gun in the field. Anxiously we waited for its appearance, saw the heads of the leaders showing in the gateway, and then realized with a sharp fear that they were stuck. Over-eagerness and the psychological effect on the drivers of being last out had resulted in their 'trying to take the gate with them'. The Major was there, directing the efforts of sweating inners and steadying the frantic horses expected to see coal-scuttle helmets coming round the corner of the crossroads.

I kept a sharp watch on the end of the lane. Should they come now, I would be their first capture, then Ross and then the whole line of guns. We stood close against hope that somehow gun would come through. And then on top of everything came the whining scream of shells, one after the other, pounding on the plateau behind us and making the horses snort in fright. In the midst of all this I became aware that someone was scrambling down the bank towards me. I whirled round to find myself confronted by a young infantry officer with two privates in attendance. He, and they, had evidently been having a rough time somewhere. His face was dirty and bloodstreaked, his uniform nearly in tatters. I realized with a shock that he was mad.

'Who are you?' he snarled, his eyes glaring, 'and where are you going?'

'A Battery, 2—th Brigade, sir, preparing to retire.' 'Retire?' he said, 'Retire?' A wan smile flickered over his face as I answered him. '*Retire?*' he repeated dreamily. 'But you can't retire. Don't you know that the German army is advancing up this slope?'

I knew only too well. 'Yes, sir.'

'Well, damn you, you must stop them!'

The glare returned. I felt very uncomfortable, and wished the Major would come along. I didn't like the way the stranger clapped the bolt of his rifle as he spoke.

'Now, come along all of you,' he continued. 'Get those rifles off the guns and climb up on the bank with my two hussars and hold the enemy. Get a move on, damn you!'

The drivers stared open-mouthed as Ross and I obeyed his orders and began slowly to unfasten the straps that held the rifles on the gun-limber. The two hussars had now posted themselves on top of the bank, but the officer stood there in the road muttering to himself. In desperation I called to him, 'What about all these guns, sir?'

His only answer was to raise his rifle till he had me covered, and I really thought he would shoot. I went on unstrapping, and had got one rifle loose when I heard the urgent gallop of hoofs and the Major's voice: 'Walk! March!'

The poor mad officer turned to meet him. I slipped the rifle back in its place, dived between the wheel and centre horses and ran round to get my own mount, with Ross close at my heels. As we moved off I turned to watch the developments. The Colonel had arrived now and was glaring at the forlorn figure in his path. I felt terribly sorry for the infantry officer, but he seemed past all reasoning with, and I had a last glimpse of him going to meet his end at the side of his two hussars on the top of the bank.

He vanished from my mind as we approached the crossroads and heard continuous whinings of bullets over our heads. We kept low on our horses. As long as the bank sheltered us it was not so bad, but at the turn there lay an open expanse in the centre of which was the crossroads. We began to trot. Behind us the ground quivered to the successive shocks of shells that smothered the plateau in black explosions.

'Trot out!'

At a fast trot that threatened to break into a gallop we rode into full view of the German armoured car that was stuck there on the road up from Flavy with its machine gun spitting and cracking at the unexpected target that had so suddenly presented itself. Faster and faster grew the pace; the noise of the guns and vehicles behind us increased to a sustained roar, and round we went with our heads down alongside the necks of our horses and the air full of eerie whistlings.

A mile down the road we eased up and finally settled down to a brisk walkout, now that the immediate danger was past. A little farther along we saw a sergeant of our B battery riding back to meet us. I thought B were through all right, but the next day I heard that they had been left behind to deal with the cavalry and that one of their gun-teams had been disabled at the crossroads by the machine gun. The sergeant had volunteered to go back and get the gun.

Very much pleased with ourselves at having got safely out of such a tight corner, we rode at ease through open, untouched country where the road wound gently around low wooded hills and dipped into pleasant valleys, wondering now and again where the Fritzes might be and how much farther we were to retire. There was no general flight on the part of the army which was in the line, or at least their flight was not visible. It was true that many bedraggled parties of infantrymen had passed through our positions that day, but apart from them we saw no great bodies of troops on the move. The reason for this I discovered later was the fact that the line had been so thinly held that when the retirement started there was hardly any one left to retire. Our own division, the Fourteenth, to which we had been attached for the last few months, seemed to be lost altogether. For the first three days of the great retreat of the Fifth Army we had seen no other artillery at all, nor had we heard any.

We were still retreating in a southerly direction, which was bringing us more and more into the French army area. As yet we had seen no French troops, but a strong rumour spread that one of their army corps was hurrying to our support and would come along at any moment. We discovered some days afterwards that they were hurrying in a totally different direction.

At four o'clock in the afternoon the brigade dropped into action in open country with the guns elevated to fire over a range of thickly wooded hills. I did not know where the enemy were, and even now I do not know. A brisk rate of firing were kept up all the evening and till long past midnight. Sleep was again denied to us; during the night we were shelled with light stuff which indicated that the enemy field batteries were not very far behind their infantry. All sorts of wild rumours were current. It was said that we were entirely surrounded and that the enemy was now in our rear and slowly closing in. We lost the desire for sleep, fidgeting about aimlessly round the guns and hoping the next move was not far off. But it was ten o'clock in the morning when the order arrived.

This time we did not travel very far back. Just over the next range of hills, descending slowly on the other side, we saw a level plain spread out before us, a plain that bore no sign of activity. It seemed that the brigade were the sole survivors of the Fifth Army in this part of the line. No help showed itself on either hand; there was just the brigade vainly trying to steady things up and escaping by the skin of its teeth from the rapidly advancing enemy, a rolling expanse of deserted country greeting us as we deployed into action again, and a sense of unreality hanging over everything.

We opened fire again on our unseen target at three o'clock in the afternoon, but not for long. Nerves were getting frayed. In the absence of information it was suicidal to delay our retirement. Cavalry might be sweeping round on the flanks. And the French had not come yet.

Another hour of the road, then action again. Six o'clock now on the 24th of March. Strung out across the low-lying fields were the silent guns, eighteen of them in a line together, with wider spaces between marking off the batteries, trained carefully on a dip in the wooded skyline in front of them. Through this small defile the enemy would most certainly appear, and the first sight of field-grey against the trees would jerk the firing levers of the whole brigade. We stared at the distant woods, and waited.

Then suddenly from behind us, from the quiet countryside,

rode forth at the gallop a magnificent line of French cavalry. We thrilled to their approach. Straight for the line they rode, passing on the right of the guns with pennons flying from erect lances and urging their horses to greater speed as they took the slope leading up to the woods ahead. They breasted the rise in open formation, drawn apart from each other somewhat but in perfect line as the fringe of the trees was reached. Now we took our gaze off them and looked behind us again, this time full expecting to see the landscape hidden by the moving masses of horizon-blue uniforms, which we had so long awaited. But there was nothing to be seen. Keenly disappointed we returned to the more hopeful sight of the single line of horsemen on the hillside. We still felt sure that they must be the advance guard of the legions to come. But even this picture had taken on a different aspect now, and the last vestiges of hope died in our hearts as we saw them turn tail at the approach to the defile and come flying back down the slope at a much greater speed than they had gone up it. We concluded sadly that they had only been retreating the wrong way and had discovered their mistake in time. Somewhere at the end of the line of guns there sounded a faint, ironic cheer as the Cuirassiers or Chasseurs or whatever they were disappeared the way they had come.

Darkness came on without the slightest sign of the enemy's appearance in the defile so carefully covered by the guns. And once it was dark it was no use waiting any longer; so about nine o'clock we took to the road again.

Through the night we rode, strangers in a strange land of great mysterious woods and silent, deserted hamlets. There was not a soul left in the villages on our line of march, the population of the countryside having abandoned everything and fled twenty-four hours before the retreating armies came rough.

What they could not carry with them they had left behind, and there were whole rows and streets of cottages with furniture in them and curtains still up at the windows, all ready to be plundered and perhaps burnt by the Jerries in a few hours' time. It seemed only right we could in order that it should not fall enemy, but strict orders were issued against looting. When darkness fell, however, we did a bit of foraging in one village, and several bottles of wine made their appearance; moreover, when we pulled into Crisolles to billet for the night, I was sure I could smell roast chicken somewhere.

Billet for the night was the order. Already it was twelve o'clock. We were not to undress but to lie down in the nearby barns with all our clothes on and the harness on the horses' backs. Our barn-load debated whether we should take off just a few of our things, and, very stupidly in view of the circumstances, we decided to undress and put our handy so that we could slip them on at once if necessary.

It became necessary at one o'clock, after we had slept like logs for a short hour. Some one burst in through the door of the barn, waking us up with excited shouts: 'Come on out of it! Jerry's in the end of the village!' A mad scramble ensued; we fought for our boots and puttees and tunics in pitch darkness, no one stopping to light a candle, then we fell over each other in our haste to be going. The battery was moving off already; our subsection sergeant was yelling himself hoarse for us to get our horses and follow; we got mounted in a hurry, with bandoliers hanging round our necks, and trotted out of the field down to the road. Everything and everybody seemed to be on the move; columns of vehicles were retiring through the village at a brisk trot, while our brigade waited to collect its stragglers and follow suit. Then we too made off in the direction of supposed safety, clearing the outskirts of Crisolles at the same time as the field-greys cautiously advanced through its streets and burnt a barn here and there to give themselves light.

Away on the right a red glow shone against the night sky; another village was being fired, perhaps a town. To the left was the blackness of great forests; everything was shrouded in silence, and the air seemed charged with suspense and uncertainty. For all we knew we were running right into their hands as the gloomy woods closed in over the road. We listened for the noises of German cavalry galloping to head us off, but the silence held.

There was some little excitement when it became known that one of the members of the battery had been left behind in Crisolles. The missing man was an NCO who had somehow failed to hear the alarm and had looked out of his deserted loft to see German infantry in the yard below him. He dropped through the window on the other side and ran for it, catching us up some hours later by sheer good luck.

Here was a crossroads, and a mounted figure, a staff officer. I could see the red tabs and the gold braid. The whole brigade halted dead behind us as the Major stopped to receive orders. Two torches played eagerly over maps at the saddlebows. Noyon, said the Major. Roye, said the staff officer, very stiffly and brusquely. That way, said the Major. This way, said the staff captain, pointing. Under no circumstances, said the Major; the line of retreat lay so-and-so and so-and-so and so on, and he would take full responsibility. A new note had come into his voice, hard and authoritative; the staff officer could do what he liked, but this particular brigade was going this way and no other way.

We drew on, leaving the staff captain with his gold braid and red tabs standing in the shadows out of our way. Good old Major!

The signposts told us that we had left Noyon behind us a little way now. Soon it would be captured, a great town full of shops and the like, now merely an incident of the night to us, a passing memory of a word on the signposts. We were concerned more with the strange noises on our left. Since leaving Crisolles we had heard them continuously, a loud rumbling of transport that seemed to be coming nearer, as though the road upon which the unknown army travelled ran parallel with our own. As the roar grew louder, one thought only filled our minds—the Jerries were cutting us off! Their road was converging upon ours, and sooner or later it would join at a fork, and we should be done for. Why didn't we trot and make a dash for it?

The Major told me then to ride back for Corporal G, hand over my horse to him and send him up ahead for orders. I did so very reluctantly; I didn't want to lose my grey, and besides it meant having to ride on the waggons or a gun-limber, which was very uncomfortable. But the mare was handed over, Corporal G galloped off to report to the Major, and we all heard him riding off alone into the darkness. Now the noise on our left was positively alarming in its closeness.

Then, suddenly, the level rumble of our own column changed to the heavier thundering of guns and waggons driving faster and faster on the echoing road. The waggon I was sitting on got under way at a rare pace, making me hold on tight to the hand rail. Round a wide bend we careered before entering on a long straight stretch which promised a gallop. And gallop we did. It was half a mile or more to the next bend, and here it was that the other road met ours, running into it from the shadows. And at a fork, bolt upright in his saddle, with rifle levelled at the livid face of a French general, sat Corporal G, holding back a whole division of flying Frenchmen that we might get out first.

Morning came while we were still on the road. The pace had dropped some hours since to a monotonous walk. We went on, half asleep in our saddles, hungry, thirsty, gnawing at mouldy bits of biscuit hunted up from our pockets, chilled through and through with the bitter wind of the March dawn. We rode through deserted hamlets and now and again a larger village, its main street crowded with the vehicles and horses of the armies in retreat with us—there were long delays while the disorder of traffic was sorted out somehow and sent on its weary way again; then we were alone once more on the road as the dawn showed us a wide view of open country. At nine o'clock, still breakfastless, we dropped into action near the village of Lagny. All day the guns kept up their barrage on the roads that we had ourselves traversed during the night. The ranges were very short; that fact we realized without caring much for its significance, for we were very tired and moved about as in a dream.

Late afternoon saw the usual spectacle of the infantry retiring. Small parties of them threaded their way past our guns, some slightly wounded, all dropping with fatigue. They asked for something to eat, but we had nothing ourselves and they carried on resignedly. Two or three of the Staffords flung themselves down by the guns, utterly worn out and unable to go any farther. From them we got news of the proximity of the German infantry, news which made us wonder why the Jerries did not make one clean sweep with their cavalry and cut off the last scattered remnants of the Fifth Army. There was no one at all in the line.

'Did you see anything of a staff officer on the road?' asked one of the infantrymen, a corporal.

'On horseback?' I remembered the staff captain.

'Yes.'

'We saw one last night trying to direct traffic. That one you mean?'

'That's the bloke. He tried to direct us, but we lynched him. He was a Jerry.'

With the disappearance of the infantry, we knew it would not be long before we, too, took the road again. Another night of travel faced us. Already we were a good forty miles from St Quentin and it looked as though we should be on the run for a few more days at least, as there seemed no sign of a stand being made anywhere. At nightfall, therefore, we limbered up to retire, and this time we trusted there was to be a sleep at the end of the march. We could not go on much longer without food or sleep.

We arrived in Thiescourt village at midnight. The rattle of the guns on the pave woke us out of our doze, and we looked around expectantly, thinking that here at last was the long-awaited billet where we should sleep for at least twenty-four hours. But the place was alive with other artillery and infantry and transport of all kinds, crowded wheel to wheel in the main square in a solid block of traffic that moved this way and that way and yet did not move at all. Behind us more and more horses and waggons poured into the village to add to the congestion. It was like a jam of logs on a Canadian river, waiting for someone to move the key-log.

Eventually we scrambled through amid the curses of those who were squeezed against our wheels as we pulled put. The bottleneck of Thiescourt, where we had been stuck for over an hour, released us into the starlit night, and we rode on again muffled up against the cold. They followed six solid hours of the road, with billets as far away as ever and the horses on the point of collapse.

Three days later there was a strange sight to be seen in a field on the outskirts of Arsy village, near to Compiegne: the sight of a whole brigade of Field Artillery, horses and men, fast asleep in full marching order. The Great Retreat, so far as we knew, was over at last; the line had been stabilized at Amiens and the threatened drive through to Paris stopped just in time.

And so we slept. From three o'clock in the afternoon until the stars came out to look at us, there on the grass we lay like drugged men, every bone in our bodies aching from the rigours of ten days and nights of rearguard actions and hasty retirements and the endless journeyings through the night, famished, unwashed, in the main street of Compiegne with only the promise of rest that afternoon keeping us from falling out of our saddles; and now we were safe at last. We slept, and slept, and slept.

ESCAPE FROM A SUNKEN SUBMARINE

T.C. Bridges and H. Hessell Tiltman

The courage and fortitude with which all these men, in the practical darkness of the slowly flooding compartment, faced a situation more than desperate, was in accordance with the very highest traditions of the Service.

These words are quoted from a report received by the Admiralty from the Commander-in-Chief of the British Fleet in Chinese waters, with regard to the loss of the submarine, Poseidon, and the whole report was read by the First Lord of the Admiralty before a crowded House of Commons on a day in July 1931. The First Lord added, amid cheers, that suitable recognition of those concerned was under consideration by the Admiralty.

The Poseidon, one of the large and powerful P Class of submarines, was built in 1929 by the firm of Armstrong-Vickers, She was two hundred-and-sixty-feet long, had a surface speed of 17.5 knots, and was fitted with eight twenty-one-inch torpedo tubes. Her displacement was one thousand four hundred and seventy five tons.

With her three sister ships, Perseus, Pandora and Proteus, she was commissioned at Barrow on 20 March 1930. She was manned equally from Portsmouth, Devonport and Chatham, and the four submarines left Portsmouth on 12 December 1930, on a fifteen-thousand-mile voyage to the eastern seas, where they were to replace vessels of the L Class. In old days submarines were always escorted on long voyages by surface ships, but these four P Class submarines were considered powerful enough to look after themselves, and voyaged without escort.

The voyage was marred by a mishap, for, when only five days out, the Proteus and the Pandora came into collision. They were, however, only slightly damaged, and were able to reach Gibraltar, where repairs were effected. The flotilla then proceeded to Chinese waters, and made its way to Weihaiwei, the naval and coaling station on the north-east coast of the Chinese province of Shantung.

On June 9, 1931, manoeuvres were being carried out, and at midday the Poseidon was about twenty-one miles out from port and some distance from the rest of the squadron when she was rammed by the steamer, Yuta. The Yuta was a British-built ship of about two thousand tons, but owned and manned by the Chinese.

The Yuta struck the Poseidon on the starboard side with such terrible force that her heavy bow drove right through the steel side of the submarine. The force of the collision rolled the submarine over, flinging every one in her off his feet, and drove her almost under water. As the Yuta reversed her propellers and drew clear, the sea poured into the breach in the Poseidon's side, and within two minutes the submarine had disappeared. At the time of the collision the submarine had been running on the surface, so fortunately her conning-tower was open and twenty-nine of the crew, including five officers, managed to scramble out, and fling themselves into the sea. These were all picked up by boats lowered by the Yuta.

The rest, trapped helplessly in the bowels of the ship, were most of them, drowned at once. The exceptions were six men, who at the time of the accident were in the forward torpedo flat. These were Petty Officer Patrick Willis, who was torpedo gunner's mate, Able-seaman Lovock, Able-seaman Holt, Able-seaman Nagle, Leading-seaman Clarke and a Chinese steward, Ah Hai.

Their feelings may be imagined when they were all flung off their balance by the deadly shock of the collision, and when they heard the screech of torn steel, all knew what had happened. From a distance came the echoed shout, 'Close watertight doors,' and all picked themselves up and sprang to obey. The bulkhead was buckled by the force of the collision, the door stuck, and it took the combined efforts of all the men to force it back into position. Willis took charge. 'Stick to it,' he told them; 'it may save the ship.' But within a few moments all knew that there was no chance of this, for the submarine lurched heavily to starboard, and she shot to the bottom with terrible speed.

It was a moment of absolute horror for the six men in that low-roofed, air-tight compartment. They were far out to sea, they knew the water was deep, but none knew exactly how deep. To make matters worse, the shock of the collision had cut off all electric lights, and they were in black and utter darkness. With a slight jar the submarine struck bottom and settled on the soft mud, luckily in an upright position. For a few moments there was complete and deadly silence; then a beam of light cut through the blackness. Willis had found an electric torch and switched it on. His first care then was for the bulkhead door. A small amount of water was leaking through, but not enough to cause alarm. The danger was from suffocation. The air in this confined space would not last six men for very long. Willis knew that although every effort would be made to reach them by the surface ships, which included the aircraft carrier, Hermes and the cruisers, Berwick and Cumberland, a considerable time must elapse before divers could descend, and he was aware that if their lives were to be saved all must depend upon their own efforts.

There was just one hope. The Poseidon, like all modern submarines, carried the Davis rescue gear. This consists of a sort of gas-mask with a coat that slips over the head. It is provided with a cylinder containing enough oxygen to last the wearer for forty-five minutes. When the tap of the oxygen cylinder is turned, the garment expands like a balloon. Wearing this apparatus, a man can rise to the surface from any depth where the pressure is not sufficient to crush him.

Then why not step out at once and go up to the top is the question which will occur to a good many of our readers.

It seems simple enough, but in point of fact the difficulties of escaping from a closed steel shell, such as that in which Willis and his companions were imprisoned, are very great. The submarine lay at the bottom of water more than one hundred feet deep, and the pressure on the hatch, which was their only way out of the compartment, was enormous. The combined muscle power of a score of men could not have lifted that hatch a single inch, and, as Willis knew, the only way in which to open it was to equalize the pressure.

Some of the men knew this as well as Willis, but others did not fully understand, so as they stood there in the thick, stuffy darkness, Willis carefully explained it to them. Then he hesitated.

'We're in a pretty tight place. Hadn't we better say a prayer, lads?' he suggested. Nods gave consent, and as all stood with bared heads, Willis uttered a brief prayer for divine help, and the others responded, 'Amen.'

Then Willis took command.

'We've no time to waste,' he said. 'I'm going to open the valves and flood the compartment.' Some one suggested that if he flooded the compartment he would drown the lot, for the water would rise over their heads, but Willis had already thought that out, and directed two of the men to rig a hawser from one side to the other, so that they could all stand on it. The Chinese boy did not understand how to put on his escape gear, so Seaman Nagle showed him the way of it. Nagle backed up Willis all the way through, and did his share towards keeping up the spirits of the rest of his companions.

The valves were opened, and water began to pore in. The six took up their positions on the hawser below the hatch and waited. Since they had but one torch and no refill, Willis switched it off so as to save light, and there they stood in Stygian blackness while the water bubbled in and rose slowly over the floor beneath them.

The air grew more and more stuffy, and after a time the man next to Willis whispered to him that he thought the oxygen in his flask was exhausted, for he could no longer hear it bubbling. Willis tested his own, and found that it, too, was empty. But he had no idea of allowing that fact to be known. Anything like panic would be fatal at this juncture.

'It's all right,' he answered, lying valiantly; 'you can't hear anything in mine, but there is plenty left.' The minutes dragged by, each seeming like an hour. It was not only the darkness but the intense silence which strained their nerves to the uttermost.

Now and then Willis switched on his torch, and glanced down at the water, which, owing to the air pressure, rose very slowly. After two hours and ten minutes had passed, the water had risen above the hawser and was up to the men's knees, then at last Willis decided that the pressure must be pretty nearly equal, and that it was time to go.

Willis's first inquiry was for Lovock and Holt, and he was saddened to hear that Lovock had come to the surface unconscious, and died almost immediately. Holt, in a state of exhaustion, had managed to support Lovock's body until both were picked up.

Willis recovered rapidly, and refused to remain in hospital a day longer than was necessary. At the beginning of September he arrived back in England, and was drafted to the torpedo training school at Portsmouth. Then he began to suffer from sleeplessness. Night after night he lived over again those agonizing hours in the black gloom of the flooded chamber at the bottom of the muddy Chinese sea. He made no complaint, but neurasthenia developed, and he was sent to Netley Hospital.

Meantime a London newspaper started a shilling subscription for the purpose of buying a home for the brave fellow. The response was immediate and generous. Money came from all parts of the country and all parts of the Empire, and a house was bought at Merton, in Surrey, and well equipped and furnished. There Patrick Willis, with his young wife and baby daughter Julia, has made his home.

Willis has left the navy and found employment in civil life. He is physically fit again, and no doubt in time his nervous system will recover from the strain to which it was subjected.

We began this chapter by quoting from the official report on the Poseidon disaster. We cannot end it better than by repeating the last sentence of that same report:

The coolness, confidence, ability and power of command shown by Petty Officer Willis, which, no doubt, was principally responsible for the saving of so many valuable lives, is deserving of the very highest praise.

AN UNDERGROUND WALK

Sylvia Green

'But, Trev, you know I *loathe* crawling about in caves!' said Judy Hamilton crossly.

She was lying on her back in the pinewoods above the Pyrenean village where she and her brother, Trevor, were spending the summer holidays.

In the hot sun of early afternoon the scent of the pines was wonderful. Judy, replete with one of Madame's splendid picnics of cold omelette and potatoes and a yard or so of French bread, drowsily sniffed it up, murmuring to herself, 'Divine!… mmmm…Divine!'

'Whatever are you snuffling about?' enquired Trev. 'Well, as I was saying, the Painted Cave is simply marvellous. It's an awful bind Marc having to go down to Perpignan to meet his father today, just when we were going to have a good scout round it…'

He paused for a comment, but Judy merely gave an inelegant grunt.

'Oh, come on, Ju, be a sport!' he urged. 'I only want to go and finish looking at the Painted Cave. It really is worth seeing. Besides, you haven't very far to go, and there's nothing grisly like slithering through a siphon. In fact it's really just a walk.'

'An underground walk,' Judy pointed out. 'And probably with bats!'

'Oh, belfries to you! Come on!'

Whether Judy would have come on had the day remained fine is doubtful, but just then a distant roll of thunder was heard from across the valley. Opening her eyes and looking upwards, she saw that some ominous clouds had come up, though they had not yet obscured the sun. She sat up reluctantly. 'Oh, well, if there's going to be a storm we might as well be in your old Painted Cave, I suppose. Though I can't think why it should choose today to rain. It hasn't rained since we've been here!'

Trev merely said, 'Good girl!' approvingly, and began collecting the debris of the picnic. 'We'll nip down to Marc's place, and dump the rucksack there and borrow a couple of torches. And then off we go!'

It did not take them long to get down to the shed in the meadow behind Marc's home where he and his father, the Professor, kept their cave-exploring equipment.

'Oughtn't we to ask if we can borrow the torches?' enquired Judy doubtfully.

'Oh, I don't think so,' said Trev, selecting two helmets and two torches. 'Besides it looks as if everyone's having a zizz.'

Below them the village was asleep in the sunshine, and there seemed no one but themselves about as they took the steep path that led up through the meadows to the cave entrance. It gave them quite a start when Le Chevrier—the idiot boy who herded the goats—popped out from behind a boulder as they came up to the cave-entrance and started gibbering at them and flinging his arms about.

'Now what d'you suppose all that means?' queried Trev. 'I expect he doesn't want us butting into his nice dry cave where he's going to shelter if it rains,' suggested Judy.

'Yep, that'll be about it.'

'Well, I wouldn't want his company either,' declared Judy. 'I think he's creepy!'

Trev chortled. 'In more ways than one, I bet! But he's quite harmless. Marc said so.'

'Maybe. But I can't do with caves and creepiness both at once, so I hope he isn't thinking of coming in with us!' But apparently he had no such intentions; when he saw they were set on going into the cave, he stopped gabbling at them and threw up his hands in a wild gesture. 'Oh, nuts to him!' said Trev and led on into the cave.

The entrance to the cave was on stepping-stones because out of its mouth flowed a small stream; but, once inside, it broadened out and there was room to walk beside the stream on a narrow beach of large water-worn stones. On the map the stream had the grandiloquent name of 'La Cataracte du Diable'—the Devil's Cataract—but Judy remarked that it was no more than an imp-sized one.

The light from the entrance lasted them for a good way in, but eventually the cave took a sharp turn and they had to put their torches on.

As Trev had promised, the journey to the Painted Cave was little more than a walk, though occasionally a rather scrambling walk over boulders, and they followed the stream all the way till it went under a narrow, shoulder-high arch. Here there was no beach, so they had to walk in the stream to get through the arch, keeping their heads well down to avoid banging them on its low rock roof. Once through the arch, they could stand upright again; indeed the cavern they were now in seemed very lofty but very narrow, and the stream turned sharply as it came out of the arch and ran away to the left through this rocky defile. In front of them was an almost perpendicular rock-wall, so Judy was turning left to follow the stream when Trev checked her.

'No, it's this way,' he said, pointing to the right. To the right there appeared to Judy to be merely a continuation of the rock-wall, but when Trev shone his torch on it she saw that it sloped steeply backwards and that, though it was perfectly smooth, someone had driven several metal footholds into it so that it could easily be climbed.

'Here, I'll go first and give you a hand up,' said Trev. 'You have to squeeze through a sort of porthole at the top and then you just drop down into the Painted Cave.'

Judy could not resist saying sarcastically. 'Of course it's really just a walk!' But, in fact, the footholds made it quite easy, and a few minutes later they were standing on the fine sand floor of a smallish cave with fairly smooth rockwalls. In the light of their torches these walls were an astonishing sight for they were alive with painted animals; there were deer and bison, reindeer and cave-bears, wild boars and wild horses, in red and brown and yellow and black, and they seemed to charge out of the walls as the beams of light swept over them.

Judy gasped. 'Are they frightfully old?' she asked.

Trev nodded. 'Ten thousand years, at least, and some of them a lot more than that.'

'They're super. How could a lot of old cavemen draw so well?' wondered Judy. 'Come on, I want to go right round and see everything.'

'Okay,' agreed Trev, much gratified by Judy's enthusiasm. They were perhaps three-quarters of the way round when they became conscious of a loud roaring noise.

'I say, is that the thunder?' exclaimed Judy.

'I shouldn't think one would hear that down here,' objected Trev.

'Then what is it?' asked Judy uneasily. And then she pointed to the porthole entrance and exclaimed, 'It's coming from just out there!'

'Give me a hitch up and I'll see.'

Judy gave him a hitch and he got his head and shoulders through the porthole and looked out. What he saw in the light of his torch appalled him. A black wall of water, so smooth as almost to seem solid, was surging down the stream-bed towards him; it hit the ramp up which they had climbed, swirling it up to within a foot or two of the porthole, and then was sucked back in a whirlpool of foam to go boiling through the low arch—which it completely filled—and so out into the outer cavern. This then was the real 'Cataracte du Diable'. He watched it horrified for a few moments, during which the black wall of water never slackened, and then dropped back white-faced into the Painted Cave.

But it did not need Trev's tell-tale face to tell Judy that something terrible had happened. The rushing of the water, magnified by the enclosed space, was now like the roar of an express train. Shouting to make herself heard, she asked in a shaking voice, 'What is it, Trev?' He shouted back a brief explanation and then, on her insistence, gave her a leg-up so that she could see for herself.

When she had seen, she asked in a stunned sort of way, 'What do we do now?'

As if trying to convince himself, Trev yelled, 'It may stop after a bit.'

'No!' cried Judy with conviction. 'No! Not with that name— it won't. Oh, Trev, whatever are we going to do?'

'We can just wait here and see if the water goes down,

or...or we can make a search for some other way out while we're waiting. Marc says there are dozens of ways out of these caves. What d'you say?'

'I'm for searching then,' shrilled Judy, though what she longed to say was, 'Do something! Do anything! We're trapped. We're caught. But let's pretend we can do something to help ourselves. If I stay still a moment longer in this horrible place, I shall go into screaming hysterics!' With trembling fingers she picked up her torch. 'Let's start in the part we haven't seen yet.'

But the rock-walls seemed absolutely solid in that part of the cave, and it was not till they had got halfway round again in a second review that Trev noticed a narrow opening at floor-level.

'I say, here's something!' he exclaimed. 'I think I'd better explore this.'

Judy was aghast. 'That little crack! Oh, Trev, you can't! You'd never get through—if there's anywhere to get through to!'

For answer Trev simply shouted, 'I'll give you a hitch up and you can tell me what the cataract's doing. If it's no different, I'm going to try this.'

They both knew from its sullen roar that it wasn't any different, but Judy obediently inspected it. And now she could not be sure that it had not crept up imperceptibly; no more than an inch or two, but, if it could do that, might it not... She dropped hastily back and mouthed, 'You win—try the crack. But I'm coming too!' As she spoke she felt absolutely sick with dread. She thought, 'I cannot—no, I cannot go into that tiny black space!' And then, 'But I must.' Trev protested, 'It'd be much better, Ju, for me to go first and see what it's like.'

'No,' persisted Judy. 'If you can go, I can go. In fact,' she added in a forlorn attempt at banter, 'anywhere you can go, I can go better. I'm not so broad in the shoulders as you.'

'Probably broader in the beam!' retorted Trev, not to be outdone in putting a good face on things. 'By the way, have you any eats on you? Wish I hadn't dumped the rucksack. There was quite a bit of picnic left in it.' They checked their pockets, but these only yielded a meagre return; Trev had half a small bar of chocolate and Judy no more than two rather sticky fruit-drops.

'Better than nothing,' commented Trev with forced cheerfulness. 'Now come on and let's streamline ourselves as much as possible. This is going to be what Marc calls, reptation. Lovely word, isn't it?'

'I think it's beastly. I suppose it means crawling about like a reptile?'

'That's about it. Now fix your torch in your helmet. And don't come in absolutely on top of me or I'll be putting my toe in your eye!'

The next few minutes were the worst that Judy could remember. The rock crack, or siphon, was just large enough to admit their bodies, and no more. Trev, who did not suffer from any fear of enclosed spaces, wriggled through fairly happily. But for Judy, in spite of her slighter form which went through more easily, every inch of the way was torture—mental torture. When Trev finally helped her out on the other side, she was trembling from head to foot with nervous reaction.

'That's a girl!' Trev commended her, and swung his torch to see what the siphon had brought them to. The slight beam of light hardly seemed to pierce the immensity of gloom in front of them. Trev's heart sank. Supposing that instead of finding a way out they were merely going deeper underground? Well, they could always turn back; meantime, the thing to do was to press on and see.

At least the vast cavern they were in had a smooth floor so

they were able to explore it fairly rapidly and they soon found a gallery leading off one corner of it. Trev, full of relief that it was not another siphon, led the way into it confidently, but the going was not good because the floor sloped down to one side and was slippery with water that dripped from the roof above. As they went on, the tilt of the floor increased so that it was hard to keep a footing on it, and then a swing of Trev's torch showed that an ominous-looking crevasse had opened at its lower edge. Suddenly there was a cry from Judy as her foot slipped and she slid down with her legs hanging over the black depths of the crevasse. Trev flung himself down to prevent himself from slipping too, and so pulled her back to safety; but her torch went down into the abyss and, with a shudder, they heard it strike the rock once and then again far below, and then the ghost of a splash echoed up to them. Very shaken, they traversed the rest of the gallery on hands and knees.

At last this nightmare progress ended on a solid rock platform, and here Trev insisted that they should stop and rest and eat their two fruit-drops. 'Seeing that I'm in need of glucose!' he announced. But Judy could not raise a smile or make a comeback to this remark.

From the platform, several caverns, which presented no particularly difficult features, led on from one to another and their spirits began to recover. Then in the last of these they could find no outlet at all except a small hole, high in one corner, which could only be reached by what looked like a smooth rock-fall. When Trev touched it, however, he found it to be a horribly glutinous kind of mud. Somehow they clawed and kicked their way up this mud-bank to the hole, and found that it led into another rock gallery, solid this time but too low to stand upright, and with a floor of jagged, upended rocks over which they must drag themselves painfully crouching.

So they went on for what seemed like hours, stumbling, creeping, crawling, often falling, through a bewilderment of galleries and caverns, some beautiful with stalactites, some full of flittering bats disturbed by the torchlight, and some in which the black silence was broken by the monotonous drip of unseen water; and nearly all of them were difficult, if not perilous, in some new and unforeseen way. Trev led on doggedly—because he must. He knew that his optimistic words about turning back were no longer true; they had long since passed the point of no return. And Judy followed where he led, struggling gamely on after him.

At last they stumbled out into what seemed to be just another vast cavern. The rock-floor was very broken, but at least they could ease the aching muscles of their backs by walking upright. They had not penetrated far into it, however, when Judy gave a deep sigh of exhaustion and flopped down on the ground, half-sitting and half-lying against an upstanding rock.

'I c-can't go any further for a b-bit, Trev,' she groaned, her teeth chattering from the deadly chill of these subterranean depths.

'Let's have a rest, then,' agreed Trev, keeping his teeth from chattering too by a great effort. He sat down beside her and asked. 'What about a bit of chocolate?'

'No, I don't want any,' said Judy indifferently.

'But you have some if you like.'

'Nope. I'll wait and have it with you later.'

'What time is it?'

Trev turned the torch on his watch, but it was smashed. 'Oh, heck! I must have bust it in one of those falls. What about yours?'

'F-forgot to put it on this—this morning...' Judy began.

And suddenly the thought of the sunlight through the little casement window of her bedroom at La Terrasse, and the smell of the pines blowing in through it as she had lain in bed that morning—was it only that morning, or days, or years ago?—was too much for her. She turned her head away from the tell-tale glimmer of the torch while the tears slid silently down her face.

Luckily, Trev didn't notice anything. He was saying, 'It must be night-time by now.' And then, 'I think, while we're resting I ought to put out the torch, Ju. Just while we're resting, you know. D'you mind?'

'No,' said Judy in a muffled voice. And then, 'But hold my hand, Trev, so that I know you're there.'

Trev didn't answer but seized her muddy, ice-cold hand in one equally chill and muddy, and held it hard. Then he switched off the torch and they were alone with the vast darkness.

So they sat for some time in silence. Judy had her eyes closed, but she could feel the blackness pressing on her eyeballs, and all the time her body shook with cold and her teeth chattered like typewriter keys. From somewhere, a chill current of air blew upon her face and dried the tears in stiff salt runlets upon her cheeks. But there was something else about this little wind, something familiar—something... Hovering, in her exhaustion, on the borders of consciousness, she spoke without knowing what she said, 'I smell pine trees.'

Trev sat bolt upright in dismay. What could this mean? Was Judy's mind wandering? 'What did you say, Ju?' he asked her anxiously.

Judy opened her eyes dreamily and lay staring upwards through the darkness that suddenly no longer seemed to weigh on her. 'I smell pine trees,' she repeated. 'And up there—up—up,

I see the sky—and a star!'

Now convinced that she was delirious, yet compelled by the strange conviction in her voice, Trev looked upwards too, straining his eyes through the darkness. And then he saw it too—a tiny prick of light far, far above them in a darkness that was by the merest fraction less solid than the surrounding blackness. And, at that, the truth flashed upon him.

'You're right, Ju!' he croaked. 'It is a star! That is the sky! We are—we must be at the bottom of that pit Marc calls "Le Grand Trou"—the Big Hole!'

'Oh, Trev, then we aren't underground any more!' whispered Judy.

'Well no. Not exactly. We're way down, but we aren't underneath.'

'I'm so glad! Oh, I'm so glad!' Judy's voice was the mere ghost of a whisper now. 'I don't mind anything with the sky up there. I don't mind—dying...' Her voice trailed away and Trev felt the cold little hand in his relax.

'Ju!' he cried desperately. 'Ju!' He fumbled for the torch and switched it on with trembling fingers and as it came on its rays fell full on the smooth face of the rock-wall beside him. In his distracted state he saw, but did not take in, what it revealed—a picture of a cart, strangely drawn with no perspective so that its wheels were spread flat, and the oxen that drew it lay flat on either side of their shaft, and little flat men ran alongside it. He swivelled the torch to light Judy's face and saw it ashen and with closed eyes. At first he had an awful fear that she was dead. 'Ju!' he called wildly. 'Ju!' She did not stir or answer; and when, with a sick feeling of dread, he shifted his fingers from her hand to her wrist, searching for her pulse, he could not at first find it. Then suddenly he found the place and, with a surge of relief, he felt it beating feebly but steadily under his fingers.

And yet what was the use? Here they were at the bottom of the 'Grand Trou'; a thousand-feet deep Marc had said it was, and unclimbable, except with steel ladders and all sorts of complicated apparatus. And no one knew they were here. How did the open sky and that tantalizing star above them help? They might just as well be under a thousand feet of solid rock. They would die anyway, of exhaustion and cold or thirst and starvation; it did not really make much odds which.

If that were so, wasn't it better that Ju was already unconscious and going the easy way. Trev dropped his head on her breast, and now his teeth chattered unrestrainedly and sobs shook him; not only for Ju, dear as she was to him, but for himself too. To be alone in the darkness; to die alone there…

But he only let go for a minute or so. Then he sat up and wiped away the tears determinedly. While there was life, there was hope. That was the truest thing anybody ever said, and he'd got to concentrate on it. He'd not got to give; he'd got to do everything he could to keep life in them for as long as possible in the hope that—in the hope that—well, better not dwell on exactly what hope; that wasn't his end of the business.

Resolutely, he set about making his puny arrangements. He checked his pockets and Judy's to see if there was any scrap of food that had been overlooked. An odd biscuit in the breast-pocket of his wind-breaker was a major find. He put it away carefully for future use, but meantime, he meticulously divided the small piece of chocolate in two and ate his share, putting Judy's by with the biscuit. There was little else he could do, except to try and conserve what strength and warmth they still had in their bodies as long as possible, and to save the torch for emergency use by putting it out in the meantime. He slid his arm under Judy and drew her into a bear-like hug, hoping thus to warm them both. And then, after only a slight hesitation, he put out the torch.

At first, after the torch went out, it was very bad there, alone in the thick darkness. Then he turned his head and looked upwards, and after a time he saw again the patch of lighter darkness that might be the sky, and the tiny prick of light that was a star. On this he fixed his eyes—and his mind. Time passed. Trev did not know whether it was hours or minutes. Perhaps he sank into sleep or unconsciousness and was roused again by some sound. Then suddenly it seemed to him that where there had been only one star there was now more than one. Then all the stars seemed to be moving, and very faintly, ricocheting down the immense rock-walls, came the echo of a human voice.

With a supreme effort Trev dragged himself back from the cold mist into which he was drifting. He sat up, fumbled in his pocket for the torch, and switched it on and signalled over and over again—SOS SOS SOS. He gathered his breath and gave one of the penetrating tremolo eagle-hawk cries that an Australian friend had taught him. It seemed to leave his lips as no more than a croak, but somehow the rocks took it up, magnifying it and hurling it up, up to the searchers on the heights above. Over and over again, Trev croaked out the call. Then, his effort made, he sank back into the grip of cold exhaustion, from which he was only half-roused as he was hoisted on to the back of a rescuer and perilously conveyed up the swaying steel ladders to safety.

Several days later a very subdued Marc sat talking to Trev in the meadows above La Terrasse. The 'Cataracte du Diable', having been in full spate for more than three days, had once more fallen to a trickle, but the devastation where it had run still showed on the hillside, not far from where they sat. Trev was still looking a bit pale, and Judy had only that day been declared out of danger. It had been a near thing, and she was still not allowed to see anyone.

'My father is very angry with me. He blames me absolutely,' admitted Marc. 'He says I should not have neglected to warn you how the Cataract can rise in an instant after rain.'

'I believe you did say something about it, you know, but I didn't take it in properly,' Trev excused him. 'But what beats me is how you knew where to come and look for us.'

'Oh, that! But it is known that the Cave of the Cataract connects with the "Grand Trou",' explained Marc.

'Yes, but how did you know we'd gone to the Cave of the Cataract in the first place?' Trev persisted.

At that moment Le Chevrier passed them driving his goats home from pasture. He pointed at Trev and then up the hill at the Cave of the Cataract, and gabbled something incomprehensible before slouching off after his flock. Marc jerked his head in the direction of the uncouth figure. 'You have him to thank for your lives,' he said soberly.

'Gosh! He saw us go in!' remembered Trev. 'In fact—wait a minute—yes, of course, he tried to stop us.'

'Yes, and then when the Cataract burst out after the storm, he rushed about looking for me—you were my friends he knew. We didn't lose a minute. But it takes time, you understand, to assemble the men and the equipment.' Trev nodded.

'What we didn't expect was to find you in the "Grand Trou". We thought we'd have to work through to the Painted Cave and get you out from there.'

'I see,' said Trev. 'By the way, I thought you said there weren't any paintings there in the "Grand Trou"? I saw a perfectly good painting there of a sort of spread-eagled cartwheels and oxen and...' But before he could get any further Marc grabbed his arm.

'What did you say? Wheels! A cart! Come to my father and tell him at once. This is what he has dreamed of for years—that he will find a rock-painting of a cart like the ones in Spain!'

Later, when an expedition to the bottom of the 'Grand Trou' had verified Trev's find, the Professor was in high feather at the proof of his favourite theory that prehistoric Frenchmen knew just as much as their prehistoric Spanish neighbours across the border. Moreover, with a Gallic flourish, he announced that the recess where the painting had been found would be named the Hamilton Recess, in honour of Judy and Trev.

But Judy was not impressed: 'Ugh, horrible place! I don't want anything to do with it ever again,' she declared. And then with the irritableness permitted to a convalescent, she added crossly, 'You know I loathe crawling about in caves, Trev, so why did you let him go and call his old cave after us!'

THE BEAST TAMER

Nikolai S. Leskov

My father was a well-known investigator for the law courts. He handled many important cases and often his work took him away from home; on these occasions, my mother and I stayed behind with the servants. In those days, Mother was still young and I was only a small boy. In fact I was barely five years old when I had the experience which I am going to tell you about.

It was during the winter, when the frost was so heavy that the sheep froze in the stables during the nights. The sparrows and the pigeons fell from the trees to the hard earth, frozen to death. At that particular time, my father's business commitments kept him in Jelec, and as he was unable to return home for Christmas, mother, anxious not to spend the festive season alone, decided to join him. Because of the bitter cold and the long journey involved, Mother did not take me with her, and instead I stayed with my aunt, her sister, who was married to a notorious land owner.

He was a rich old man, but a man without mercy. His character was ruled by hardness and cruelty; and, far from being ashamed, he would boast of these qualities. In his opinion, such characteristics were the proof of manly strength and unbending courage. He raised his children with unrelenting firmness and strict discipline. I was the same age as one of his sons.

Many people feared my uncle, but no one more than I, for he used his merciless strictness to force me to be brave. I remember well, how once, when I was only three years old and very frightened of a fierce thunderstorm, my uncle pushed me on to the balcony and locked me out, to cure me of my fear.

So you can imagine how reluctant and afraid I was to return to this household, to stay, but being so young I was not consulted, and, in fact, had no say in the matter.

On my uncle's estate stood a huge building, that looked like a castle. It was an imposing, but unattractive, one-storied house, with a dome and a tower about which many gruesome, and terrifying tales were told. Once it had been occupied by the demented father of the present owner, who had made drugs and medicines. For some reason even this was considered horrific. The greatest source of fear, however, was caused by what went on in the very top of the tower, where, across a high, paneless window, harp strings were tightly sprung. This was called Aeol's harp. When the wind played upon the strings of this capricious instrument, it made the weirdest noise, changing from a quiet, haunting whisper into an uneasy, plaintive wail, and then turning into a shrill, deafening roar. It sounded as if a whole crowd of persecuted spirits, maddened with terror, were caught in the harp's strings.

No one in the whole household could bear to hear the eerie sounds of the harp. But they all thought that this instrument gave orders to its hard-hearted master, and that this accounted for his merciless cruelty. Everyone was well aware that when thunder raged in the night and the harp screeched so piercingly that it was heard all over the village, its lord and master would be unable to sleep and would rise in the morning, ill-tempered and frowning. He would issue impossible orders to his servants, who would be dreadfully nervous and frightened all day.

It was the custom of this household that no crime or misdeed ever went unpunished, and there were no exceptions to this rule. It applied to one and all—human beings, animals, even insects. My uncle showed no mercy, hating the very word, as to him it was a mark of weakness. He preferred to be ruthless and unforgiving, and would not tolerate any form of leniency. It was therefore not surprising that his household and all the villages which belonged to his large, wealthy estate, were overshadowed by gloom and sadness, which even spread to the animals.

Uncle's greatest love was to go on a hunt with his dogs. He hunted wolves, hares and foxes with his greyhounds, and he raised a special breed of dogs for bear hunting. These were called leecher-dogs, probably because once their sharp teeth fastened themselves into the bear's flesh, they would cling to the beast like leeches, refusing to let go. Sometimes the bear crushed them with one blow of his massive paw, or tore the hound in half, but the leecher-dog would never let go while it was still living and breathing.

Nowadays different methods are used for baiting the bears, and this particular breed of dogs no longer exists in Russia, but at the time of which I am talking, leecher-dogs were always present in a good hunting party. Many bears used to roam this part of the country, and the bear hunt always provided excitement and amusement.

Whenever the hunters found a bear's lair with cubs, they would take them alive and bring them back home. Usually they kept the cubs in a large, stone outhouse, where the tiny windows were built high under the roof. Thick, heavy bars spanned the windows and the only way the bear cubs could reach them, was by standing one on top of the other and by clinging to the bars with their claws. This was the only way they could get a glimpse at the world outside their prison. Before lunch, we always went for a walk, and we liked to go past the outhouse to see the claws of the comical cubs protruding from the windows. Our German tutor, Kolberg, sometimes gave them pieces of bread saved from breakfast, on the end of a stick.

The bears were placed in the charge of young Ferapont, who also took care of the kennels. I remember him well; he was a young man of medium height, and about twenty-five years old. He was muscular, strong and daring. Everyone thought him to be very handsome with his white complexion, red cheeks, thick locks of black, curly hair and enormous, deep eyes. Quite apart from his good looks, he was very brave.

Ferapont had a sister called Anna, who used to come to help our nurse, and she told us many interesting stories about her brother's bravery and his unusual friendship with the bears. Summer and winter alike, Ferapont slept with the beasts inside their outhouse. They would lie all around him, and often would use his head or a shoulder as a cushion. Colourful flower gardens stretched in front of Uncle's house, surrounded by ornamental fencing that had wide gates in the centre. A tall, smooth pole stood on a green lawn, beyond these gates, and we called this the Perch of the Privileged. At the very top of the pole a small shelter had been firmly fixed.

It was the custom to choose the most intelligent and dependable bear from the captured cubs, and allow it to move quite freely in the gardens and parks. But the privileged beast was assigned a special duty—namely to be on guard by the pole in front of the gates. So it would spend most of its time there, either relaxing on the lawn under the pole or else, having climbed up the pole into the shelter, dozing or sleeping undisturbed by people or hounds.

Only the exceptionally tame and the exceptionally wise bears were allowed to live such a free existence, and their liberty ended abruptly as soon as they showed their natural animal instincts. As long as they took no notice of chickens, geese, calves and of people, they were safe. But the bear who disturbed the peace of the inhabitants, or showed his true animal nature by turning into a hunter, was immediately sentenced to death and nothing could save him.

Such an unfortunate bear would be thrown into a deep pit in a field between the village and the forest. After a few days, a long wooden plank would be pushed into the hollow and he would be forced to climb out. As soon as the bear appeared, my uncle's leecher-dogs would pounce upon him. If these hounds proved no match for the bear, failing to kill him, and there was a danger that he might escape into the forest, two expert huntsmen would take up the hunt; they would set a pair of the most experienced and vicious hounds on to the beast to finish him.

If by some freak of nature however, even these skilful dogs could not kill the bear or prevent him from breaking through to the small area of woodland connected to the thick forests, then an experienced marksman would come forward with his long, heavy, Kuchenreiter rifle, to fire the deadly shot into the bear's heart.

It seemed impossible for a bear to escape all these dangers, but if, by some chance he did get away, the consequences for those involved with the hunt would have been terrible. Their punishment would have been death. The selection of the most trustworthy cub was left to Ferapont, because he spent so much time among them and because he was considered something of an expert. He was warned he would be held responsible if he made a bad choice, but he did not hesitate and chose a bear cub who was amazingly clever and wise. Nearly all the bears in Russia are called Myshka, but this bear was called Sganarel, which is a most unusual Spanish name. Sganarel grew from a cub into a big, healthy bear of tremendous strength. He was also quite handsome and quite an acrobat. With his short round nose and a graceful, slight figure, he was more like a giant poodle or a bloodhound than a bear. His hind quarters were rather skinny, with short, shiny fur, but he had the most magnificent, broad chest and back, which was covered with thick, long fur. He was quick-witted and learnt many tricks, which was unusual for an animal of his breed. For example, he could walk forward and backwards on his hind legs quite easily, he could play the drum, and march with a stick carved in the shape of a gun under his arm. Sganarel was also always happy and willing to help the peasants carry their heavy sacks to the mill. For such trips, he would cheekily put a wide-rimmed straw hat with a peacock's feather on his head.

But the fateful day came when the strong natural animal instincts overpowered even the good-natured, friendly Sganarel. Shortly before my arrival at Uncle's house, the no longer dependable Sganarel was found guilty of several lapses, which got progressively worse.

The things he did wrong were typical of his breed. First, he tore a wing off a goose; then, he placed his paw upon the spine of a young foal and broke its back; and finally, he took a dislike to a blind beggar and his guide, and rolled them over and over in the snow, hurting their hands and legs so badly they had to be taken to hospital. At this point, Ferapont was ordered to lead Sganarel into the pit; the pit which had only one way out, and that was the way to the execution.

That evening, when Anna was putting my cousin and me to bed, she told us how sad and touching it was when her brother took Sganarel to the pit to await the killing. Ferapont did not even have to put rings through his mouth, nor use iron chains; it had not been necessary to take the bear by force. As soon as Ferapont said, 'Come with me, bear,' the trusting beast got up and followed him. Funnily enough he even placed his old straw hat upon his head, and put his arm around Ferapont's waist as they walked towards the concealed pit, so they looked just like a pair of good friends.

And that is exactly what they were. Ferapont felt dreadfully sorry for his furry friend, but there was no way in which he could help him. I must remind you, that in the district where this happened, it was unknown for anyone to be forgiven for any wrongdoing, so now the degraded Sganarel had to pay for his misdemeanours with his life.

It was decided the killing should take place during the afternoon, to amuse the numerous visitors who had gathered as usual at uncle's house to spend Christmas with him. The order for the preparation of the bear-baiting had gone out the minute Ferapont had left to put the guilty Sganarel into the pit.

It was easy to make the bears walk into the pits, which were usually camouflaged by brushwood thrown on top of thin branches strewn across the opening. Then this roof was covered with snow. The trap was so well disguised, the bears were unaware of danger. They were taken to the edge of the pit and then—one or two more paces—and the unsuspecting animals fell into the deep hollow, from which it was impossible to escape. They had no other choice but to await their terrible fate.

When the time came for the chase and the killing, a narrow plank, five metres long, was placed in the pit for the bear to climb out. If by any chance the beast was clever enough to sense the danger and refused to come up, he was prodded with long, spiked rods, handfuls of burning straw were thrown upon him, or blank cartridges were fired into the pit, to force him out.

When Ferapont had left Sganarel inside his deep, cold prison, he was feeling terribly unhappy and sad. Unfortunately he confided in his sister, telling her how friendly the bear's behaviour had been towards him, how willingly he accompanied him to the trap and that, when he finally fell through the brushwood to the bottom of the pit, he squatted upon his hind quarters, put his front paws together as if he was pleading, and whimpered pitifully.

Ferapont also told Anna how he had run away from the pit, because his heart could not bear to hear Sganarel's heart-rending cries.

'Thank God it is not my task to shoot him, if he starts to run towards the woods,' he sighed. 'I could not carry out such an order, I would rather undergo the greatest torture, than shoot Sganarel,'

Anna told us all this, and we in turn told our tutor, Kolberg. In an effort to amuse Uncle, Kolberg passed the whole story on to him. Uncle said, 'We shall test that fellow Ferapont,' and clapped his hands three times. This was the signal to summon his valet—Ustin Petrovich—an old Frenchman, who had been in Uncle's service since his capture many years before. Ustin Petrovich, or Justin, as he was called for short, entered the room, wearing his purple valet's cloak with the gold buttons. Uncle ordered him to inform the celebrated Flegont, the famous marksman who never missed his target, and Ferapont, that they would be the selected pair of riflemen. It would be their duty to hide in the woods and kill the doomed bear if he tried to escape during the chase. Uncle probably hoped to be further entertained by watching the terrible struggle by the unfortunate man between his loyalty to his master and his love for the beast. If Ferapont refused to fire upon Sganarel, or if he purposely missed when firing, he would be punished ruthlessly and the bear would be slain with the second shot from Flegont, who was not only acurate, but perfectly reliable. As soon as this order had been given and Justin had left the room, we children realized what a terrible thing we had done. If only we had not repeated what we had heard! Only God knew how this nightmare would end. We were so upset, that though we had not eaten for the whole day, we failed to enjoy the delicious Christmas Eve feast, which began the moment the first star lit up the sky. We did not even take an interest in the other children among the guests, and continually worried about Sganarel and Ferapont; unable to make up our minds which one of them we pitied the most.

My cousin and I tossed and turned in our bed late into the night. When we finally fell asleep, our bad dreams about Ferapont and Sganarel made us restless and we slept fitfully. The nurse, not understanding, tried to comfort us by saying we need not be frightened of the bear, as he was secure in the pit and would be killed the next day. I was even more upset and disturbed at this.

I even asked the nurse if I could pray for Sganarel, but such a question was above the old woman's religious understanding. She yawned, made the sign of the cross and said she didn't know about that, that she had never asked her spiritual father such a question, but that the bear was, after all, also one of God's creatures, who had found shelter on Noah's Ark.

Christmas day finally arrived and, all dressed up in our Sunday best, we were waiting to take tea with our tutors and governesses. The drawing room was packed with relatives and other guests; including the priest, the deacon and two choir soloists from our church. When Uncle entered, the representatives of the church raised their voices with: 'Jesus Christ was born today.' Then everyone drank tea, which was followed by a small breakfast and, at two o'clock, we sat down to a festive dinner.

As soon as the meal was over, everybody went quickly to get ready to watch Sganarel's killing. They had to hurry, for dusk descends swiftly at that time of the year, and it would have been impossible to proceed with the bear-baiting in darkness, when the bear could easily escape from sight.

Everything went according to plan. So we would not miss a thing, we rushed to dress straight from the dinner table. Wrapped in our warm, rabbit-fur coats, and shod in high, furry boots with thick, goat-skin soles, we were taken outside and placed in one of the sledges. By the gates stood a line of luxurious, roomy sledges, padded with colourful carpets and warm rugs, and each harnessed to a team of horses. Two grooms held the reins of Uncle's high-spirited English hunting horse, Monden. At last Uncle came out, wearing a fox-skin fur coat and a fur pointed cap. As soon as he had mounted his horse and sat astride his bearskin saddle decorated with snake heads, our long procession started to move. Ten or fifteen minutes later, we reached the chosen scene for the proceedings and, forming a semicircle, came to a halt. All the sledges were turned to face the wide, snow-covered field, which was surrounded by the chain of huntsmen on horseback. The wood formed a border at the far side of the field. Near the trees, behind some bushes, Flegont and Ferapont were hidden in trenches.

No one could see their hiding-places; only a few sharpsighted people pointed to the hardly visible gun rests, supporting the heavy rifles of the marksmen. One of these rifles was to shoot Sganarel...

As the bear's pit was also out of our sight, we gazed with at the magnificent huntsmen; who all carried very imposing-looking rifles of Swedish, German and English makes.

Uncle positioned himself at the head of his company. He held the leads of the most vicious pair of leecher-dogs, and in front of him, upon the ornate saddle, a white scarf had been placed.

The young dogs, for whom the baiting of Sganarel would be a part of their training, were present in great numbers. They lacked discipline and showed their burning impatience and craving for blood. They barked, and whined, jumping up constantly, disturbing the horses and their uniformed riders, who cracked their whips in an effort to make the young, restless hounds behave. Everyone was now impatient for the chase to begin. The dogs, of course, with their highly developed sense of smell, were well aware of the nearness of the beast and longed to pounce upon it.

It was time to bring Sganarel out from the pit and to give him to the bloodthirsty hounds. Uncle waved the white scarf and shouted, 'Begin!'

Ten riders came forward out of the main group of the huntsmen and galloped across the field. After about two hundred paces, they stopped and took hold of a long, wooden plank which, being so far away, we could not see. They were now right by the pit where Sganarel was imprisoned, but this was also out of sight.

The men lifted the plank and pushed one end down into the pit, placing it at such an angle, that the beast would have no difficulty in climbing out.

The top part of the plank was placed against the edge of the pit and we could just see the tip of it sticking out into the air.

All eyes were glued to these preparations, for they were the overture to the real drama to come. Everyone expected that Sganarel would emerge fairly quickly, but he obviously sensed what was to come and remained well out of sight.

The riders tried to force him out by bombarding him with balls and prodding him with sharp, spiked poles; loud cries were heard, but Sganarel did not appear. The sound of blank shots fired into the pit echoed into the air, but even this did not force the animal out into the open. Sganarel growled crossly, but remained firmly where he was. Before long a battered, horse-pulled sledge sped into the field. Normally it was used for manure, but now it contained a load of dry, brittle straw. The horse was tall and emaciated, as were all the horses kept to carry heavy loads from the fields. But although he was worn and old and looked half-starved, he raced with his tail high and his mane flying. Maybe his friskiness was caused by the remembered high spirits of his lost youth. I think, however, that his nervous agility was more likely to have been brought on by the sheer terror which had seized him when he sensed the bear's nearness. He darted across the white surface with such frenzy, that the driver had great difficulty in steering him in a straight line; he pulled the reins tighter and tighter, till the horse's head was forced right back, and the rough iron bit under his tongue cut his mouth and made it bleed. All the time the whip lashed mercilessly into the frightened animal's hide.

The three separate piles of straw were set alight and thrown down into the pit from three sides, so that the only part which was not burning, was the small area by the bottom end of the plank. The air exploded with the deafening, furious roar and frenzied cries from the maddened animal, but still he did not climb to the surface. We heard rumours that Sganarel had been badly burnt, and that he had covered his eyes with his paws and was cowering in a corner, where no one could get at him.

The old nag with the torn mouth galloped away from the pit. Thinking that he had been sent for another load of hay, some of the spectators complained in whispers. Why, they asked, had not the organizers of the chase ordered a larger load of hay in the first place, so that there would have been some to spare? Uncle looked angry and was shouting crossly, but I was unable to hear the words, for there was a great deal of commotion. People were talking loudly, the dogs were snarling and barking even more frantically, and the crack of the whips whistled through the air.

Then, suddenly, the mood changed; the crowds grew quiet again, as the old nag, snorting heavily, was racing back towards the deep hollow. But the sledge was not carrying the expected second load of straw; it was bringing Ferapont, the bear's friend. My furious uncle had given the order for Ferapont to be lowered into the pit, to lead out his four-legged friend to his execution. Ferapont seemed very agitated, but he acted firmly and without hesitation. He carried out his master's orders to the letter. Taking a piece of rope which had been used for tying the hay from the sledge, he fastened it securely round a notch in the plank. Then, taking the free end of the rope into his hand, he descended into the pit.

Sganarel's dreadful cries stopped and changed into muffled

grumbling, rather as if he was complaining to his friend about the cruel behaviour of the people. Eventually all was quiet.

'He is embracing and licking Ferapont!' shouted somebody, standing by the edge of the pit. Some of the spectators inside their sledges sighed, while others frowned. Many of them suddenly felt sorry for the bear and they no longer found pleasure in the thought of the killing. But such fleeting sentiments were swiftly pushed out of mind by the next unexpected, frightful development.

Ferapont's curly head emerged from the pit as he climbed upwards along the plank, with the aid of the rope. He was not alone; Sganarel, locked in a fond embrace with his friend, his furry head upon Ferapont's shoulder, was coming up close behind him. The bear was clearly unhappy and looked a very sorry sight. He looked exhausted and hurt, and we felt this to be caused not so much by his physical suffering, but more by the shock of his morale. The angry gleam of his blood-shot eyes reflected his anger and irritation, and his whole appearance reminded us of King Lear.

His fur was dishevelled, scorched in places and knotted with blades of straw. And, like King Lear, Sganarel too, had his own kind of a crown.

The bear had refused to be parted from his old straw hat, and had been wearing it when he was led into the pit. Perhaps it was just a coincidence or perhaps it was because Sganarel really treasured this gift from his beloved friend; but whatever the reason, he was still clutching the battered straw hat as he came out into the open. As he stood once again upon solid ground, momentarily secure and content in the nearness of his friend, he took the crushed, battered hat from under his arm and put it on his head.

Many of the crowd saw the funny side of this scene and roared with laughter, but others, as they watched the beast, were filled with a sudden surge of compassion. Some of them even turned their backs to the spectacle, no longer wanting to witness the cruel ending. While all this was going on, the leecher-dogs forgot completely the meaning of the word obedience; snarling and growling they jumped up with vicious frenzy. The whips no longer had any effect upon them. As soon as the young hounds and the old experienced leecher-dogs saw Sganarel come out of the pit, they nearly suffocated as they strained at their iron collars. By then Ferapont was speeding in the old sledge back to his hiding-place near the edge of the wood.

Once again Sganarel was left alone. He was jerking his paw with some impatience, for it was caught up in the rope fastened to the plank. He obviously wanted to release his paw from the loop so he could run after his friend, but even the most intelligent bear is still only a bear, and Sganarel, instead of managing to loosen the loop, merely tightened it even further.

When he realized his efforts were getting him nowhere, he tugged at the rope with all his strength to try and break it, but it was exceptionally strong and held fast. The movement had jerked the plank from its original position, and Sganarel looked towards the pit to see what was happening. Just then, two leecher-dogs, released from the pack, pounced upon his back and the sharp teeth of one bit deeply into his flesh. Sganarel had been so preoccupied with the rope, that the hounds had taken him completely by surprise; at first, he was more surprised by their audacity, than angry; but a second or two later, when the leecher-dog extracted its teeth so it could sink them even deeper into his flesh, the bear tore the dog from his back and flung it away from him with such force, it slit its stomach. The white snow where the hound landed was marked immediately with a pool of fresh blood. With one sharp blow of his back paw, the bear then crushed the body of the second dog.

But the most amazing and frightening thing of all was what happened with the plank. When Sganarel hurled the first leecher-dog into the air, the powerful movement pulled the plank right out of the pit. It flew upwards, the rope, to which it was still attached, became taut, and then the long piece of wood started to circle round and round Sganarel, as if he was its axis. The far end of the plank skimmed the snowy ground, knocking down and crushing not just a dog or two, but a full pack of hounds. Some whimpered with pain, their paws jerking in the snow, others turned over and remained motionless and silent.

Either the bear was of such exceptional intelligence that he realized he held the deadliest weapon—or the rope was cutting into his paw and inflicting pain, but he let out a warlike roar, seized the rope even more firmly with his paw and swung it even more ferociously. The powerful weapon swished through the air, knocking down all that stood in its way. If, God forbid, the rope had snapped, the plank would have soared away from its axis, bringing utter destruction to all alive and breathing in its path.

All of us, who were grouped together on the field—the spectators, the huntsmen, the horses and the hounds—were now placed in great danger and we prayed that the rope wrapped around Sganarel's paw would remain intact. But how would it all end? Most of us were no longer interested. With the exception of the two marksmen hidden by the wood, and a handful of huntsmen, the rest of the crowd turned away from the scene, very much afraid, and ordered their drivers to race with the wind from this dangerous place. They flew back to the house in panic and commotion.

Because of this hasty retreat and the resulting chaos, several slight crashes and falls occurred along the route, causing some laughter and some alarm. Those who fell out of the sledges into the snow were quite sure that they could see the plank whistling over their heads and the outraged beast racing towards them. The guests, who returned to the house, were able to calm down, but to those who remained at the scene of the chase, the horror was not yet at an end.

It was impossible to set other dogs upon Sganarel. It was clear to everybody watching, that as he was so adequately armed, he would be capable of mowing down all the packs of hounds without any damage to himself. So the bear, without interference, continued to swing the plank round and round, turning with it at the same time; and made his way towards the wood, unaware that death was waiting for him there. Ferapont, and the infallible marksman, Flegont, were ready for him in their separate hiding-places.

One accurate shot was all that was needed to end it all. But it seemed that fate was on Sganarel's side, for it intervened again to save the bear's life.

Just when Sganarel neared the barriers, behind which the two marksmen were taking aim with just the muzzles of their guns showing, the rope suddenly snapped, and the plank flew sideways like an arrow fired from a bow. The bear lost his balance and fell over in the snow.

The handful of spectators left on the field were in for yet another surprise. The plank, in its flight, knocked down the gun rest and the barrier which was protecting Flegont, then it shot over his head and became embedded in a distant snow-drift. Sganarel also did not waste his time. He rolled over and over in the snow, till he landed behind Ferapont's barrier.

Recognizing his good friend, he breathed on him with his hot breath and began to lick him all over. Just then there was the sound of a shot from the direction of Flegont's hideout, but it was Ferapont who fell unconscious to the ground, while the bear ran off into the woods, unhurt.

People rushed over to Ferapont to see how badly he was hurt; the bullet had struck his hand and passed right through it. A few stray hairs from Sganarel's fur were lodged in the wound.

Flegont's reputation for excellent marksmanship did not really suffer. The circumstances had forced him to shoot in haste and without using the gun rest. Daylight too had been failing fast and Ferapont and the bear were standing very closely together. In fact under such unfavourable conditions, it was a wonder the shot struck so near to its intended target.

Nevertheless Sganarel had escaped and it was futile to pursue him in the gathering dusk. By the time the following day began, their lord and master, whose word was law, had very different thoughts, from the chase, on his mind.

As the chase had such an unsatisfactory ending, Uncle returned home angrier and more ill-humoured then ever. Even before dismounting his horse, he was issuing orders to track the beast down at sunrise and to surround him in such a manner that an escape would be impossible.

A properly conducted hunt would surely have a better result than the afternoon's fiasco. All of us were wondering and worrying what punishment would be given to the poor wounded Ferapont, and it was the general opinion that a cruel fate would be in store for him. He had, after all, committed a crime by not plunging his hunting knife into the bear's heart when he had the chance, and by allowing him to escape unhurt from the hideout. The suspicion that during that fateful moment Ferapont had purposely refused to raise his hand against his furry friend and had deliberately sent him off to freedom, was more damning still. It seemed very likely that Ferapont had chosen to be loyal to Sganarel, for their firm friendship was common knowledge.

We children listened to the discussions of the grown-ups, who had gathered that evening in the spacious drawingroom, where the tall, beautifully decorated and illuminated Christmas tree was the centre of attraction. And, like our elders, we too were worried about Ferapont.

A rumour reached us from the hall, and quickly spread through the whole room, that as yet no decision had been made as to what was to be done with Ferapont.

'Can this be a good, or a bad omen?' someone whispered, and this whisper made us even more anxious and miserable.

Father Alexei, the old village priest, had also heared the muffled question. He sighed deeply and murmured, 'Let us pray to Jesus.'

Then he made the sign of the Cross, and all those present followed his example—relatives, guests, free men, serfs, rich men, poor men and children alike. It was the right time to pray for help. Before our arms had fallen back to our sides, the doors opened and Uncle entered, a walking stick in hand, his two favourite hounds at his heel. Justin followed him, carrying his pipe and the ornate tobacco pouch on a silver tray.

Uncle's carved armchair stood on a Persian rug in the centre of the room, right in front of the Christmas tree. In silence he sat down, and in silence he took his pipe and pouch from his valet. The hounds settled themselves at his feet, stretching their long noses on the carpet.

Uncle was wearing a silk, dark-blue dressing-gown, beautifully and heavily embroidered. His hand clutched the thin, but strong walking stick, made from the branch of a Caucasian cherry-tree.

He was using the walking stick, for during the recent panic at the bear-baiting, his frisky mount, Monden, had also been nervous; the horse had reared wildly, and side-stepped, pressing Uncle's leg against a tree. The injury caused him severe pain and made him limp slightly. We thought that such an incident could only add fire to his anger and fury. The fact that we all remained perfectly and utterly silent after his arrival in the room also did not help matters, because, like so many suspicious people, Uncle detested silence. Father Alexei, who knew Uncle well, hastened forward to break the ominous hush and to save the situation as best as he could. As we children had gathered around him, he turned to us, asking if we knew the meaning of the hymn: 'Our Saviour is Born'. It soon became obvious, that not only us young ones, but many of the grown-ups did not understand the words fully. The priest then went on to explain the true significance of phrases such as 'Praise Him', 'Welcome Him' and 'Lift up your hearts and souls'.

As the Father talked of the last expression, he quietly and simply offered his heart and soul to God. And he told us about the gift which now, as always, even the poorest beggar can offer to Baby Jesus. This gift would be more precious than the presents of gold, frankincense and myrrh, brought to him by the wise men from the East. We could offer him our hearts, bettered and reformed by his teaching. The elderly priest talked of love, mercy and forgiveness, of the duty of each one of us to help and comfort friend and foe alike 'in the name of Christ'.

His words were sincere and convincing, and we all listened

intently, in the profound hope that they would reach the heart and soul of the one for whom we knew they were intended. Tears of compassion were glistening in many eyes.

Something fell to the floor with a clatter. It was Uncle's cane. Someone picked it up and handed it back, but Uncle did not touch it; instead he sat, slumped to one side, a hand hanging limply over the arm of the chair. His forgotten pipe slid from his grasp, but no one rushed forth to pick it up. Instead everyone's gaze was glued upon his face, for something unbelievable was happening: Uncle was crying!

The priest quietly stepped through the circle of us children, walked up to Uncle and silently blessed him. Uncle raised his head, clasped the frail Father by his hand, kissed it fervently in front of us all and whispered, 'Thank you.' Then he turned to Justin and ordered him to bring Ferapont to him. Ferapont appeared and stood in front of Uncle, white-faced, and with a bandaged hand.

'Stand over here!' Uncle commanded, pointing to the Persian rug, directly in front of his feet. Ferapont obeyed and fell to his knees. 'Rise!...on your feet!' Uncle said. 'I forgive you.'

Ferapont once again fell to his knees, but Uncle spoke to him in a strange, passionate voice, 'You gave a beast deeper love than many of us are capable of giving another human being. Your loyal affection has moved me to generosity. To show my admiration, I am giving you your freedom and one hundred roubles for your journey. Go to wherever you wish.'

'Thank you, but I shall not go away!' Ferapont said.

'What is it that you want?' his master asked.

'Because you have shown me kindness, I wish to remain with you; I will serve you more faithfully now when I am a free man, than when I was a serf under your rule of terror.'

Uncle dabbed his eyes with his white handkerchief, then, leaning forward, embraced Ferapont; all of us present also stood up and there was not a dry eye amongst us. We could not help but feel that the Lord's name had been praised in this very room, and that a reign of happiness and peace had taken over from the former reign of terror.

The good news spread into the village with the barrels of mead, which were sent as a token of goodwill. Soon the sky was lit with the glow of fires, as merriment and happiness entered every heart. People said to one another, 'This Christmas even the beast has celebrated the birth of our Christ.'

They did not search for Sganarel in the forest. Ferapont, as he was promised, was given his freedom, and before long took over Justin's duties to become not just a faithful servant, but also a trusted friend. When Uncle died, it was Ferapont who closed his eyes for the last time and who buried his remains in the Vagankov cemetery in Moscow. A memorial in his honour stands there to this very day, and there, by Uncle's feet, lies Ferapont.

No one places flowers upon their resting-place now, but in some far corners of Moscow there are still some people left who remember the erect, white-haired man, who had the gift of recognizing true sorrow and who was always ready to help. Sometimes he sent his good, faithful servant to help the needy; but neither of them ever came empty-handed. These two good people, about whose deeds so much more could be told, were my uncle and his loyal servant Ferapont, whom the old master jokingly called: 'the Beast Tamer'.

THE ISLE OF VOICES (HAWAII)

R.L. Stevenson

Keola was married to Lehua, daughter of Kalamake, the wise man of Molokai, and he kept his dwelling with the father of his wife. There was no man more cunning than that prophet; he read the stars, he could divine by the bodies of the dead, and by means of evil creatures: he could go alone into the highest parts of the mountain, into the region of the hobgoblins, and there he would lay snares to entrap the spirits of the ancient. For this reason, no man was more consulted in all the kingdom of Hawaii. Prudent people bought, and sold, and married, and laid out their lives by his counsels; and the King had him sent twice to Kona to seek the treasures of Kamehameha. Neither was any man more feared: of his enemies, some had dwindled in sickness by the virtue of his incantations, and some had been spirited away, the life and the clay both, so that folk looked in vain for so much as a bone of their bodies. It was rumoured that he had the art or the gift of the old heroes. Men had seen him at night upon the mountains, stepping from one cliff to the next; they had seen him walking in the high forest, and his head and shoulders were above the trees.

This Kalamake was a strange man to look at. He came of the best blood in Molokai and Maui, of a pure descent; and yet, he was more white to look upon than any foreigner; his hair the colour of dry grass, and his eyes red and very blind, so that 'Blind as Kalamake that can see across tomorrow,' was a byword in the islands.

Of all these doings of his father-in-law, Keola knew a little by common repute, a little more he suspected, and the rest he ignored. But there was one thing that troubled him. Kalamake was a man that spared for nothing, whether to eat or to drink, or to wear; and for all he paid in bright new dollars. 'Bright as Kalamake's dollars,' was another saying in the Eight Isles. Yet he neither sold, nor planted, nor hired—only now and then for his sorceries—and there was no source conceivable for so much silver.

It chanced one day, Keola's wife was gone upon a visit to Kaunakakai on the lee side of the island, and the men were at the sea, fishing. But Keola was an idle dog, and he lay in the verandah and watched the surf heat on the shore and the birds fly about the cliff. It was the chief thought with him always— the thought of the bright dollars. When he lay down to bed, he would be wondering why they were so many, and when he woke at morn, he would be wondering why they were all new; and the thing was never absent from his mind. But this day of all days, he resolved of some discovery.

For he had observed the place where Kalamake kept his treasure, which was a lockfast desk against the parlour wall, under the print of Kamehameha the Fifth, and a photograph of Queen Victoria with her crown; and no later than the night before, he found occasion to look in, and behold! The bag lay there empty. And this was the day of the steamer; he could see her smoke off Kalaupapa; and she must soon arrive with a month's goods, tinned salmon and gin, and all manner of rare luxuries for Kalamake.

'Now if he can pay for his goods today,' Keola thought, 'I shall know for certain that the man is a warlock, and the dollars come out of the devil's pocket.'

While he was so thinking, there was his father-in-law behind him, looking vexed.

'Is that the steamer?' he asked.

'Yes,' said Keola. 'She has but to call at Pelekunu, and then she will be here.'

'There is no help for it then,' returned Kalamake, 'and I must take you in my confidence, Keola, for the lack of anyone better. Come here within the house.'

So they stepped together into the parlour, which was a very fine room, papered and hung with prints, and furnished with a rocking chair, and a table and a sofa in the European style. There was a shelf of books beside, and a family Bible in the midst of the table, and the lockfast writing desk against the wall; so that any one could see it was the house of a man of substance.

Kalamake made Keola close the shutters of the windows, while he himself locked all the doors and set open the lid of the desk. From this, he brought forth a pair of necklaces hung with charms and shells, a bundle of dried herbs, and the dried leaves of trees, and a green palm branch.

'What I am about,' said he, 'is a thing beyond wonder. The men of old were wise; they wrought marvels, and this among the rest; but that was at night, in the dark, under fit stars and in the desert. The same will I do here in my own house, and under the plain eye of day.' So saying, he put the Bible under the cushion of the sofa so that it was all covered, brought out from the same place a mat of a wonderfully fine texture, and heaped the herbs and leaves on sand in a tin pan. And then, he and Keola put on the necklaces, and took their stand upon the opposite corners of the mat.

'The time comes,' said the warlock, 'be not afraid.'

With that he set flame to the herbs, and began to mutter and wave the palm. At first the light was dim because of the closed shutters; but the herbs caught strongly afire, and the flames beat upon Keola, and the room glowed with the burning; and next, the smoke rose and made his head swim and his eyes darken, and the sound of Kalamake muttering ran in his ears. And suddenly, to the mat on which they were standing came a snatch or twitch, that seemed to he more swift than lightning. In the same wink the room was gone, and the house, the breath all beaten from Keola's body. Volumes of sun rolled upon his eyes and head, and he found himself transported to a beach, under a strong sun, with a great surf roaring: he and the warlock standing there on the same mat, speechless, gasping, and grasping at one another, and passing their hands before their eyes.

'What was this?' cried Keola, who came to himself the first, because he was the younger. 'The pang of it was like death.'

'It matters not,' panted Kalamake. 'It is now done.'

'And, in the name of God, where are we?' cried Keola.

'That is not the question,' replied the sorcerer. 'Being here, we have a matter that we must attend to. Go, while I recover my breath, into the borders of the wood, and bring me the leaves of such and such a herb, and such and such a tree, which you will find to grow there plentifully—three handfuls of each. And be speedy. We must be home again before the steamer comes; it would seem strange if we had disappeared.' And he sat on the sand and panted.

Keola went up the beach, which was of shining sand and coral, strewn with singular shells; and he thought in his heart:

'How do I not know this beach? I will come here again and gather shells.'

In front of him was a line of palms against the sky; not like the palms of the Eight Islands, but tall and fresh and beautiful, and hanging out withered fans like gold among the green, and he thought in his heart:

'It is strange I should not have found this grove. I will come here again, when it is warm, to sleep.' And he thought, 'How warm it has grown suddenly!' For it was winter in Hawaii, and the day had been chilly. And he thought also, 'Where are the grey mountains? And where is the high cliff with the hanging forest and the wheeling birds?' And the more he considered, the less he could conceive in what quarter of the islands he was fallen.

In the border of the grove, where it met the beach, the herb was growing, but the tree farther back. Now, as Keola went towards the tree, he was aware of a young woman who had nothing on her body but a belt of leaves.

'Well!' thought Keola, 'they are not very particular about their dress in this part of the country.' And he paused, supposing she would observe him and escape; and seeing that she still looked before her, stood and hummed aloud. Up she leaped at the sound. Her race was ashen; she looked this way and that, and her mouth gaped with the terror of her soul. But it was a strange thing that her eyes did not rest upon Keola.

'Good day,' said he. 'You need not be so frightened, I will not eat you.' And he had scarce opened his mouth before the young woman fled into the bush.

'These are strange manners,' thought Keola, and, not

thinking what he did, ran after her.

As she ran, the girl kept crying in some speech that was not practised in Hawaii, yet some of the words were the same, and he knew she kept calling and warning others. And presently he saw more people running—men, women, and children, one with another, all running and crying like people at a fire. And with that he began to grow afraid himself, and returned to Kalamake bringing the leaves. Him he told what he had seen.

'You must pay no heed,' said Kalamake. All this is like a dream and shadows. All will disappear and be forgotten.'

'It seemed none saw me,' said Keola.

'And none did,' replied the sorcerer. 'We walk here in the broad sun invisible by reason of these charms. Yet they hear us; and therefore, it is well to speak softly, as I do.'

With that he made a circle round the mat with stones, and in the midst he set the leaves.

'It will be your part,' said he, 'to keep the leaves alight, and feed the fire slowly. While they blaze (which is but for a little moment) I must do my errand; and before the ashes blacken, the same power that brought us carries us away. Be ready now with the match; and call me in good time lest the flames burn out and I be left.'

As soon as the leaves caught, the sorcerer leaped like a deer out of the circle, and began to race along the beach like a hound that has been bathing. As he ran, he kept stooping to snatch shells; and it seemed to Keola that they glittered as he took them. The leaves blazed with a clear flame that consumed them swiftly; and presently, Keola had but a handful left, and the sorcerer was far off, running and stopping.

'Back!' cried Keola. 'Back! The leaves are nearly done.'

At that Kalamake turned, and if he had run before, now

he flew. But fast as he ran, the leaves burned faster. The flame was ready to expire when, with a great leap, he bounded on the mat. The wind of his leaping blew it out; and with that the beach was gone, and the sun and the sea; and they stood once more in the dimness of the shuttered parlour, and were once more shaken and blinded; and on the mat betwixt them lay a pile of shining dollars. Keola ran to the shutters; and there was the steamer tossing in the swell close in.

The same night Kalamake took his son-in-law apart, and gave him five dollars in his hand.

'Keola,' said he, 'if you are a wise man (which I am doubtful of) you will think you slept this afternoon on the verandah, and dreamed as you were sleeping. I am a man of few words, and I have for my helpers people of short memories.'

Never a word more said Kalamake, nor referred again to that affair. But it ran all the while in Keola's head—if he were lazy before, he would now do nothing.

'Why should I work,' thought he, 'when I have a father-in-law who makes dollars of seashells?'

Presently his share was spent. He spent it all upon fine clothes. And then he was sorry:

'For,' thought he, 'I had done better to have bought a concertina, with which I might have entertained myself all day long.' And then he began to grow vexed with Kalamake.

'This man has the soul of a dog,' thought he. 'He can gather dollars when he pleases on the beach, and he leaves me to pine for a concertina! Let him beware: I am no child, I am as cunning as he, and hold his secret.' With that he spoke to his wife Lehua, and complained of her father's manners.

'I would let my father be,' said Lehua. 'He is a dangerous man to cross.'

'I care not for him!' cried Keola; and snapped his fingers. 'I have him by the nose. I can make him do what I please.' And he told Lehua the story.

But she shook her head.

'You may do what you like,' said she; 'but as sure as you thwart my father, you will be no more heard of. Think of this person, and that person; think of Hua, who was a noble of the House of Representatives, and went to Honolulu every year; and not a bone or a hair of him was found. Remember Kamau, and how he wasted to a thread, so that his wife lifted him with one hand. Keola, you are a baby in my father's hands; he will take you with his thumb and finger and eat you like a shrimp.'

Now Keola was truly afraid of Kalamake, but he was vain too; and these words incensed him.

'Very well,' said he, 'if that is what you think of me, I will show how much you are deceived.' And he went straight to where his father-in-law was sitting in the parlour.

'Kalamake,' said he, 'I want a concertina.'

'Do you, indeed?' asked Kalamake.

'Yes,' said he, 'and I may as well tell you plainly, I mean to have it. A man who picks up dollars on the beach can certainly afford a concertina.'

'I had no idea you had so much spirit,' replied the sorcerer. 'I thought you were a timid, useless lad, and I cannot describe how much pleased I am to find I was mistaken. Now I begin to think I may have found an assistant and successor in my difficult business. A concertina? You shall have the best in Honolulu. And tonight, as soon as it is dark, you and I will go and find the money.'

'Shall we return to the beach?' asked Keola.

'No, no!' replied Kalamake; 'you must begin to learn more

of my secrets. Last time I taught you to pick shells; this time I shall teach you to catch fish. Are you strong enough to launch Pili's boat?'

'I think I am,' returned Keola. 'But why should we not take your own, which is afloat already?'

'I have a reason which you will understand thoroughly before tomorrow,' said Kalamake. 'Pili's boat is the better suited for my purpose. So, if you please, let us meet there as soon as it is dark; and in the meanwhile, let us keep our own counsel, for there is no cause to let the family into our business.'

Honey is not more sweet than was the voice of Kalamake, and Keola could scarce contain his satisfaction.

'I might have had my concertina weeks ago,' thought he, 'and there is nothing needed in this world but a little courage.'

Presently after he spied Lehua weeping, and was half in a mind to tell her all was well.

'But no,' thinks he; 'I shall wait until I can show her the concertina; we shall see what the chit will do then. Perhaps she will understand in the future that her husband is a man of some intelligence.'

As soon as it was dark, father and son-in-law launched Pili's boat and set the sail. There was a great sea, and it blew strong from the leeward; but the boat was swift and light and dry, and skimmed the waves. The wizard had a lantern, which he lit and held with his finger through the ring; and the two sat in the stern and smoked cigars, of which Kalamake always had a provision, and spoke like friends of magic and the great sums of money which they could make by its exercise, and what they should buy first, and what second; and Kalamake talked like a father.

Presently he looked all about, and above him at the stars, and back at the island, which was already three parts sunk under the sea, and he seemed to consider ripely his position.

'Look!' says he, 'There is Molokai already far behind us, and Maui like a cloud; and by the bearing of these three stars I know I have come to where I desire. This part of the sea is called the Sea of the Dead. It is in this place extraordinarily deep, and the floor is all covered with the bones of men, and in the holes of this part gods and goblins keep their habitation. The flow of the sea is to the north, stronger than a shark can swim, and any man who shall here be thrown out of a ship, it bears away like a wild horse into the uttermost ocean. Presently he is spent and goes down, and his bones are scattered with the rest, and the gods devour his spirit.'

Fear came on Keola at the words, and he looked, and by the light of the stars and the lantern, the warlock seemed to change.

'What ails you?' cried Keola, quick and sharp.

'It is not I who am ailing,' said the wizard; 'but there is one here very sick.'

With that he changed his grasp upon the lantern, and, behold—as he drew his finger from the ring, the finger stuck and the ring was burst, and his hand was grown to be the bigness of three.

At that sight Keola screamed and covered his face.

But Kalamake held up the lantern.

'Look rather at my face!' said he—and his head was huge as a barrel; and still he grew and grew as a cloud grows on a mountain, and Keola sat before him screaming, and the boat raced on the great seas.

'And now,' said the wizard, 'what do you think about that concertina? Are you sure you would not rather have a flute? No?' says he; 'that is well, for I do not like my family to be changeable of purpose. But I begin to think I had better get out of this paltry boat, for my bulk swells to a very unusual degree, and if we are not the more careful, she will presently be swamped.'

With that he threw his legs over the side. Even as he did so, the greatness of the man grew thirtyfold and fortyfold as swift as sight or thinking, so that he stood in the deep seas to the armpits, and his head and shoulders rose like a high isle, and the swell beat and burst upon his bosom, as it beats and breaks against a cliff. The boat ran still to the north, but he reached out his hand, and took the gunwale by the finger and thumb, and broke the side like a biscuit, and Keola was spilled into the sea. And the pieces of the boat the sorcerer crushed in the hollow of his hand and flung miles away into the night.

'Excuse me for taking the lantern,' said he; 'for I have a long wade before me, and the land is far, and the bottom of the sea uneven, and I feel the bones under my toes.'

And he turned and went off walking with great strides; and as often as Keola sank in the trough, he could see him no longer; but as often as he was heaved upon the crest, there he was striding and dwindling, and he held the lamp high over his head, and the waves broke white about him as he went.

Since first the islands were fished out of the sea, there was never a man so terrified as Keola. He swam indeed, but he swam as puppies swim when they are cast in to drown, and knew not wherefore. He could but think of the hugeness of the swelling of the warlock, of that face which was great as a mountain, of those shoulders that were broad as an isle, and of the seas that beat on them in vain. He thought, too, of the concertina, and shame took hold upon him; and of the dead men's bones, and fear shook him.

Of a sudden, he was aware of something dark against the

stars that tossed, and a light below, and a brightness of the cloven sea; and he heard the speech of men. He cried out loud and a voice answered; and in a twinkling the bows of a ship hung above him on a wave like a thing balanced, and swooped down. He caught with his two hands in the chains of her, and the next moment was buried in the rushing seas, and the next hauled on hoard by seamen.

They gave him gin and biscuits and dry clothes, and asked him how he came where they found him, and whether the light which they had seen was the lighthouse, Lae o Ka Laau. But Keola knew white men are like children and only believe their own stories; so about himself he told them what he pleased, and as for the light (which was Kalamake's lantern), he vowed he had seen none.

This ship was a schooner bound for Honolulu, and then to trade in the low islands; and by a very good chance for Keola she had lost a man off the bowsprit in a squall. Keola dared not stay in the Eight Islands. Word goes round so quickly, and all men are so fond to talk and carry news, that if he hid in the north end of Kauai or in the south end of Kau, the wizard would have wind of it before a month, and he must perish. So he did what seemed the most prudent, and shipped sailor in place of the man who had been drowned.

In some ways, the ship was a good place. The food was extraordinarily rich and plenty, with biscuits and salt beef every day, and pea soup and puddings made of flour and suet twice a week, so that Keola grew fat. The captain also was a good man, and the crew no worse. The trouble was the mate, who was the most difficult man to please, and who beat and cursed him daily, both for what he did and what he did not. The blows that he dealt were very sure, for he was strong; and the words he used were very unpalatable, for Keola was come of a good family and accustomed to respect. And what was the worst of all, whenever Keola found a chance to sleep, there was the mate awake and stirring him up with a rope's end. Keola saw it would never do; and he made up his mind to run away.

They were about a month out from Honolulu when they made land. It was a fine starry night, the sea was smooth as well as the sky fair; it blew a steady trade; and there was the island on their weather bow, a ribbon of palm trees lying flat along the sea. The captain and the mate looked at it with the night glass, and named the name of it, and talked of it, beside the wheel where Keola was steering. It seemed it was an isle where no traders came. By the captain's way, it was an isle besides where no man dwelt; but the mate thought otherwise.

'I don't give a cent for the directory,' said he. 'I've been past here one night in the schooner *Eugenie,* it was just such a night as this; they were fishing with torches, and the beach was thick with lights like a town.'

'Well, well,' says the captain, 'it's steep-to, that's the great point; and there ain't any outlying dangers, by the chart, so we'll just hug the lee side of it. Keep her ramping full, don't I tell you!' he cried to Keola, who was listening so hard that he forgot to steer.

And the mate cursed him, and swore that Kanaka was for no use in the world, and if he got started after him with a belaying pin, it would be a cold day for Keola.

And so the captain and mate lay down on the house together, and Keola was left to himself.

'This island will do very well for me,' he thought; 'if no traders deal there, the mate will never come. And as for Kalamake, it is not possible he can ever get as far as this.'

With that he kept edging the schooner nearer in. He had to do this quietly, for it was the trouble with these men, and above all with the mate, that you could never be sure of them; they would all be sleeping sound, or else pretending, and if a sail shook, they would jump to their feet and fall on you with a rope's end. So Keola edged her up little by little, and kept all drawing. And presently, the land was close on board, and the sound of the sea on the sides of it grew loud.

With that, the mate sat up suddenly upon the house.

'What are you doing?' he roars. 'You'll have the ship ashore!'

And he made one bound for Keola, and Keola made another clean over the rail and plump into the starry sea. When he came up again, the schooner had payed off on her true course, and the mate stood by the wheel himself and Keola heard him cursing. The sea was smooth under the lee of the island; it was warm besides, and Keola had his sailor's knife, so he had no fear of sharks. A little way before him the trees stopped; there was a break in the line of the land like the mouth of a harbour; and the tide, which was then flowing, took him up and carried him through. One minute he was without, and the next within, he floated there in wide shallow water, bright with ten thousand stars, and all about him was the ring of the land with its string of palm trees. And he was amazed, because this was a kind of island he had never heard of.

At first he sought everywhere and found no man; only some houses standing in a hamlet, and the marks of fires. But the ashes of the fires were cold and the rains had washed them away; and the winds had blown, and some of the huts were overthrown. It was here he took his dwelling; and he made a fire drill, and a shell hook, and fished and cooked his fish, and climbed after green cocoa nuts, the juice of which he drank, for in all the isle there was no water. The days were long to him, and the nights terrifying. He made a lamp of cocoa shell, and drew the oil off the ripe nuts, and made a wick of fibre; and when evening came, he closed up his hut, and lit his lamp, and lay and trembled until morning. Many a time, he thought in his heart he would have been better off in the bottom of the sea, his bones rolling there with the others.

All this, while he kept by the inside of the island, for the huts were on the shore of the lagoon, and it was there the palms grew best, and the lagoon itself abounded with good fish. And to the outer side he went once only, and he looked but once at the beach of the ocean, and came away shaking. For the look of it, with its bright sand, and strewn shells, and strong sun and surf, went sore against his inclination.

'It cannot be,' he thought, 'and yet it is very like. And how do I know? These white men, although they pretend to know where they are sailing, must take their chance like other people. So that after all, we may have sailed in a circle, and I may be quite near to Molokai, and this may be the very beach where my father-in-law gathers his dollars.'

So after that he was prudent, and kept to the land side.

It was perhaps a month later, when the people of the place arrived—filling six great boats. They were a fine race of men, and spoke a tongue that sounded very different from the tongue of Hawaii, but so many of the words were the same that it was not difficult to understand. The men besides were very courteous, and the women very towardly; and they made Keola welcome, and built him a house, and gave him a wife; and what surprised him the most, he was never sent to work with the young men.

A cause of alarm for him was his wife. He was in doubt

about the island, and he might have been in doubt about the speech, of which he had heard so little when he came there with the wizard. But about his wife there was no mistake conceivable, for she was the same girl that ran from him crying in the wood. So he had sailed all this way, and might as well have stayed in Molokai; he had left home and his wife and all his friends for no other cause but to escape his enemy, and the place he had come to was that wizard's hunting ground, the place where he had walked invisible. It was at this period when he kept the most close to the lagoon side, and, as far as he dared, in the cover of his hut.

The second cause of alarm was talk he had heard from his wife and the chief islanders. Keola himself said little. He was never so sure of his new friends, for he judged they were too civil to be wholesome, and since he had grown better acquainted with his father-in-law, the man had grown more cautious. So he told them nothing of himself, but only his name and descent, and that he came from the Eight Islands, and what fine islands they were; and about the king's palace in Honolulu, and how he was a chief friend of the king and the missionaries. But he put out many questions and learned much. The island where he was, was called the Isle of Voices; it belonged to the tribe, but they made their home upon another, three hours' sail to the southward. There they lived and had their permanent houses, and it was a rich island, where there were eggs and chickens and pigs, and ships came trading with rum and tobacco. It was there the schooner had gone after Keola deserted; there, too, the mate had died, like the fool of a man as he was. It seems, when the ship came, it was the beginning of the sickly season in that isle, when the fish of the lagoon are poisonous, and all who eat of them swell up and die. The mate was told of it; he saw the boats preparing, because in that season the people leave that island and sail to the Isle of Voices; but he was a fool of a white man, who would believe no stories but his own, and he caught one of these fish, cooked it and ate it, and swelled up and died, which was good news to Keola. As for the Isle of Voices, it lay solitary the most part of the year, only now and then a boat's crew came for copra, and in the bad season, when the fish at the main isle were poisonous, the tribe dwelt there in a body. It had its name from a marvel, for it seemed the sea side of it was all beset with invisible devils; day and night you heard them talking with one another in strange tongues; day and night little fires blazed tip and were extinguished on the beach; and what was the cause of these doings no man might conceive. Keola asked them if it were the same in their own island where they stayed, and they told him no, not there; nor yet in any other of the hundred isles that lay all about them in that sea; but it was a thing peculiar to the Isle of Voices. They told him also that these fires and voices were ever on the sea side and in the seaward fringes of the wood, and a man might dwell by the lagoon two thousand years (if he could live so long) and never be in any way troubled; and even on the seaside the devils did no harm if left alone. Only once a chief had cast a spear at one of the voices, and the same night he fell out of a cocoa nut palm and was killed.

Keola thought a good bit. He saw he would be all right when the tribe returned to the main island, and right enough where he was, if he kept by the lagoon, yet he had a mind to make things righter if he could. So he told the high chief he had once been in an isle that was pestered the same way, and the folk had found a means to cure that trouble.

'There was a tree growing in the bush there,' says he, 'and

it seems these devils came to get the leaves of it. So the people of the isle cut down the tree wherever it was found, and the devils came no more.'

They asked what kind of a tree this was, and he showed them the tree of which Kalamake burned the leaves. They found it hard to believe, yet the idea tickled them. Night after night, the old men debated it in their councils, but the high chief (though he was a brave man) was afraid of the matter, and reminded them daily of the chief who cast a spear against the voices and was killed, and the thought of that brought all to a stand again.

Though he could not yet bring about the destruction of the trees, Keola was well pleased, and began to look about him and take pleasure in his days; and, among other things, he was kinder to his wife, so that the girl began to love him greatly. One day he came to the hut, and she lay on the ground lamenting.

'Why,' said Keola, 'what is wrong with you now?' She declared it was nothing.

The same night she woke him. The lamp burned very low, but he saw by her face she was in sorrow.

'Keola,' she said, 'put your ear to my mouth that I may whisper, for no one must hear us. Two days before the boats begin to be got ready, go you to the seaside of the isle and lie in a thicket. We shall choose that place beforehand, you and I; and hide food; and every night I shall come near by there singing. So when a night comes and you do not hear me, you shall know we are clean gone out of the island, and you may come forth again in safety.'

The soul of Keola died within him.

'What is this?' he cried. 'I cannot live among devils. I will not be left behind upon this isle, I am dying to leave it.'

'You will never leave it alive, my poor Keola,' said the girl; 'for to tell you the truth, my people are eaters of men; but this they keep secret. And the reason they will kill you before we leave is because in our island ships come, and Donat-Kimaran comes and talks for the French, and there is a white trader there in a house with a verandah, and a catechist. Oh, that is a fine place indeed! The trader has barrels filled with flour; and a French warship once came in the lagoon and gave everybody wine and biscuit. Ah, my poor Keola, I wish I could take you there, for great is my love to you, and it is the finest place in the seas except Papeete.'

Now Keola was the most terrified man in the four oceans. He had heard tales of eaters of men in the south islands, and the thing had always been a fear to him; and here it was knocking at his door. He had heard besides, by travellers, of their practices, and how when they are in a mind to eat a man, they cherish and fondle him like a mother with a favourite baby. And he saw this must be his own case; and that was why he had been housed, and fed, and wived, and liberated from all work; and why the old men and the chiefs discoursed with him like a person of weight. So he lay on his bed and railed upon his destiny; and the flesh curdled on his bones.

The next day, the people of the tribe were very civil, as their way was. They were elegant speakers, and they made beautiful poetry, and jested at meals, so that a missionary must have died laughing. It was little enough Keola cared for their fine ways; all he saw were the white teeth shining in their mouths, and his gorge rose at the sight; and when they were done eating, he went and lay in the bush like a dead man.

The next day it was the same, and then his wife followed him.

'Keola,' she said, 'if you do not eat, I tell you plainly you will be killed and cooked tomorrow. Some of the old chiefs are murmuring already. They think you are fallen sick and must lose flesh.'

With that Keola got to his feet, and anger burned in him. 'It is little I care one way or the other,' said he. 'I am between the devil and the deep sea. Since die I must, let me die the quickest way; and since I must be eaten at the best of it, let me rather be eaten by hobgoblins than by men. Farewell,' said he, and he left her standing, and walked to the sea side of that island.

It was all bare in the strong sun; there was no sign of man, only the beach was trodden, and all about him as he went, the voices talked and whispered, and the little fires sprang up and burned down. All tongues of the earth were spoken there: French, Dutch, Russian, Tamil, Chinese. Whatever land knew sorcery, there were some of its people whispering in Keola's ear. That beach was thick as a fair, yet no man seen; and as he walked he saw the shells vanish before him, and no man to pick them up. I think the devil would have been afraid to be alone in such company; but Keola was past fear and courted death. When the fires sprang up, he charged for them like a bull. Bodiless voices called to and fro; unseen hands poured sand upon the flames; and they were gone from the beach before he reached them.

'It is plain Kalamake is not here,' he thought, 'or I must have been killed long since.'

With that he sat him down in the margin of the wood, for he was tired, and put his chin upon his hands. The business before his eyes continued; the beach babbled with voices, and the fires sprang up and sank, and the shells vanished and were renewed again even while he looked.

'It was a by-day when I was here before,' he thought, 'for it was nothing to this.'

And his head was dizzy with the thought of these millions and millions of dollars, and all these hundreds and hundreds of persons culling them upon the beach, and flying in the air higher and swifter than eagles.

'And to think how they have fooled me with their talk of mints,' says he, 'and that money was made there, when it is clear that all the new coins in all the world is gathered on these sands! But I will know better the next time!' said he.

And at last, he knew not very well how or when, sleep fell on Keola, and he forgot the island and all his sorrow.

Early the next day, before the sun was yet up, a bustle woke him. He awoke in fear, for he thought the tribe had caught him napping; but it was no such matter. Only, on the beach in front of him, the bodiless voices called and shouted one upon another, and it seemed they all passed and swept beside him up the coast of the island.

'What is afoot now?' thinks Keola. And it was plain to him it was something beyond ordinary, for the fires were not lit nor the shells taken, but the bodiless voices kept posting up the beach, and hailing and dying away; and others following, and by the sound of them these wizards should be angry.

'It is not me they are angry at,' thought Keola, 'for they pass me close.'

As when hounds go by, or horses in a race, or city folk coursing to a fire, and all men join and follow after, so it was now with Keola; and he knew not what he did, nor why he did it, but there, lo and behold! he was running with the voices.

So he turned one point of the island, and this brought him in view of a second; and there he remembered the wizard trees to have been growing by the score together in a wood. From this point, there went up a hubbub of men crying not to be described; and by the sound of them, those that he ran with shaped their course for the same quarter. A little nearer, and there began to mingle with the outcry, the crash of many axes. And at this a thought came at last into his mind that the high chief had consented; that the men of the tribe had set to cutting down these trees; that word had gone about the isle from sorcerer to sorcerer, and these were all now assembling to defend their trees. Desire of strange things swept him on. He posted with the voices, crossed the beach, and came into the borders of the wood, and stood astonished. One tree had fallen, others were part hewed away. There was the tribe clustered. They were back to back, and bodies lay, and blood flowed among their feet. The hue of fear was on all their faces; their voices went up to heaven, shrill as a weasel's cry.

Have you seen a child when he is all alone and has a wooden sword, and fights, leaping and hewing with the empty air? Even so the man-eaters huddled back to back and heaved up their axes and laid on, and screamed as they laid on, and behold! no man to contend with them! Only here and there Keola saw an axe swinging over against them without hands; and time and again a man of the tribe would fall before it, clove in twain or burst asunder, and his soul sped howling.

For a while Keola looked upon this prodigy like one that dreams, and then fear took him by the midst as sharp as death, that he should behold such doings. Even in that same flash the high chief of the clan spied him standing, and pointed and called out his name. Then the whole tribe saw him also, and their eyes flashed, and their teeth clashed.

'I am too long here,' thought Keola, and ran farther out of

the wood and down the beach, not caring whither.

'Keola!' said a voice close by upon the empty sand.

'Lehua! Is that you?' he cried, and gasped, and looked in vain for her; but by eyesight he was stark alone.

'I saw you pass before,' the voice answered; 'but you would not hear me. Quick! Get the leaves and the herbs, and let us flee.'

'You are there with the mat?' he asked.

'Here, at your side,' said she. And he felt her arms about him. 'Quick! The leaves and the herbs, before my father can get back!'

So Keola ran for his life, and fetched the wizard fuel; and Lehua guided him back, and set his feet upon the mat, and made the fire. All the time of its burning, the sound of the battle towered out of the wood; the wizards and the man-eaters hard at fight; the wizards, the viewless ones, roaring out aloud like bulls upon a mountain, and the men of the tribe replying shrill and savage out of the terror of their souls. And all the time of the burning, Keola stood there and listened, and shook, and watched how the unseen hands of Lehua poured the leaves. She poured them fast, and the flame burned high, and scorched Keola's hands; and she speeded and blew the burning with her breath. The last leaf was eaten, the flame fell, and the shock followed, and there were Keola and Lehua in the room at home.

Now, when Keola could see his wife at last he was mighty pleased, and he was mighty pleased to be home again in Molokai and sit down beside a bowl of *poi*—for they made no *poi* on board ships, and there was none in the Isle of Voices—and he was out of the body with pleasure to be clean escaped out of the hands of the eaters of men. But there was another matter not so clear, and Lehua and Keola talked of it all night and were troubled. There was Kalamake left upon the isle. If, by the blessing of God, he could but stick there, all were well; but should he escape and return to Molokai, it would be an ill day for his daughter and her husband. They spoke of his gift of swelling and whether he could wade that distance in the seas. But Keola knew by this time where that island was—and that is to say, in the Low or Dangerous Archipelago. So they fetched the atlas and looked upon the distance in the map, and by what they could make of it, it seemed a far way for an old gentleman to walk. Still, it would not do to make too sure of a warlock like Kalamake, and they determined at last to take counsel of a white missionary.

So the first one that came by, Keola told him everything. And the missionary was very sharp on him for taking the second wife in the low island; but for all the rest, he vowed he could make neither head nor tail of it.

'However,' says he, 'if you think this money of your father is ill-gotten, my advice to you would be to give some of it to the lepers and some to the missionary fund. And as for this extraordinary rigmarole, you cannot do better than keep it to yourselves.'

But he warned the police at Honolulu that, by all he could make out, Kalamake and Keola had been coining false money, and it would not be amiss to watch them.

Keola and Lehua took his advice, and gave many dollars to the lepers. And no doubt the advice must have been good, for from that day to this, Kalamake has never more been heard of. But whether he was slain in the battle by the trees, or whether he is still kicking his heels upon the Isle of Voices, who shall say?

THE HOLLOW MAN

Thomas Burke

He came up one of the narrow streets which lead from the docks, and turned into a road whose farther end was gay with the light of London. At the end of this road he went deep into the lights of London, and sometimes into its shadows, farther and farther away from the river; and did not pause until he had reached a poor quarter near the centre.

He was a tall, spare figure, wearing a black mackintosh. Below this could be seen brown dungaree trousers. A peaked cap hid most of his face; the little that was exposed was white and sharp. In the autumn mist that filled the lighted streets, as well as the dark, he seemed a wraith; and some of those who passed him looked again, not sure whether they had indeed seen a living man. One or two of them moved their shoulders, as though shrinking from something.

His legs were long, but he walked with the short, deliberate steps of a blind man, though he was not blind. His eyes were open, and he stared straight ahead; but he seemed to see nothing and hear nothing.

Neither the mournful hooting of sirens across the black water of the river nor the genial windows of the shops in the big streets near the centre drew his head to the right or left. He walked as though he had no destination in mind, yet constantly, at this corner or that, he turned. It seemed that an unseen hand was guiding him to a given point, of whose location he was himself ignorant.

He was searching for a friend of fifteen years ago, and the unseen hand, or some dog-instinct, had led him from Africa to London, and was now leading him, along the last mile of his search, to a certain little eating-house. He did not know that he was going to the eating-house of his friend Nameless, but he did know, from the time he left Africa, that he was journeying towards Nameless, and he now knew that he was very near to Nameless.

Nameless didn't know that his old friend was anywhere near him, though, had he observed the conditions that evening, he might have wondered why he was sitting up an hour later than usual. He was seated in one of the pews of his prosperous little workmen's dining-rooms—a little gold-mine his wife's relations called it—and he was smoking and looking at nothing.

He had added up the till and written the copies of the bill of fare for next day, and there was nothing to keep him out of bed after his fifteen hours' attention to business. Had he been asked why he was sitting up later than usual, he would first have answered that he didn't know that he was, and would then have explained, in default of any other explanation, that it was for the purpose of having a last pipe. He was quite unaware that he was sitting up and keeping the door unlatched because a long-parted friend from Africa was seeking him and slowly approaching him, and needed his services.

He was quite unaware that he had left the door unlatched at that late hour—half-past eleven—to admit pain and woe.

But even as many bells sent dolefully across the night from

their steeples their disagreement as to the point of half-past eleven, pain and woe were but two streets away from him. The mackintosh and dungarees and the sharp white face were coming nearer every moment.

There was silence in the house and in the streets; a heavy silence, broken, or sometimes stressed, by the occasional night-noises—motor horns, back-firing of lorries, shunting at a distant terminus. That silence seemed to envelop the house, but he did not notice it. He did not notice the bells, and he did not even notice the lagging step that approached his shop, and passed—and returned—and passed again—and halted. He was aware of nothing save that he was smoking a last pipe, and he was sitting in that state of hazy reverie which he called thinking, deaf and blind to anything not in his immediate neighbourhood.

But when a hand was laid on the latch, and the latch was lifted, he did hear that, and he looked up. And he saw the door open, and got up and went to it. And there, just within the door, he came face to face with the thin figure of pain and woe.

To kill a fellow-creature is a frightful thing. At the time the act is committed, the murderer may have sound and convincing reasons (to him) for his act. But time and reflection may bring regret; even remorse; and this may live with him for many years. Examined in wakeful hours of the night or early morning, the reasons for the act may shed their cold logic, and may cease to be reasons and become mere excuses.

And these naked excuses may strip the murderer and show him to himself as he is. They may begin to hunt his soul, and to run into every little corner of his mind and every little nerve, in search of it. And if to kill a fellow-creature and to suffer the recurrent regret for an act of heated blood is a frightful thing, it is still more frightful to kill a fellow-creature and bury his body deep in an African jungle, and then, fifteen years later, at about midnight, to see the latch of your door lifted by the hand you had stilled and to see the man, looking much as he did fifteen years ago, walk into your home and claim your hospitality.

When the man in mackintosh and dungarees walked into the dining-rooms, Nameless stood still; stared; staggered against a table; supported himself by a hand, and said 'Oh!'

The other man said, 'Nameless!'

Then they looked at each other; Nameless with head thrust forward, mouth dropped; eyes wide; the visitor with a dull, glazed expression. If Nameless had not been the man he was—thick, bovine and costive—he would have flung up his arms and screamed. At that moment he felt the need of some such outlet, but did not know how to find it. The only dramatic expression he gave to the situation was to whisper instead of speak.

Twenty emotions came to life in his head and spine, and wrestled there. But they showed themselves only in his staring eyes and his whisper. His first thought, or rather, spasm, was 'Ghosts—Indigestion—Nervous—Breakdown.' His second, when he saw that the figure was substantial and real, was 'Impersonation'. But a slight movement on the part of the visitor dismissed that.

It was a little habitual movement which belonged only to that man; an unconscious twitching of the third finger of the left hand. He knew then that it was Gopak. Gopak, a little changed, but still, miraculously, thirty-two. Gopak, alive, breathing and real. No ghost. No phantom of the stomach. He was as certain of that as he was that fifteen years ago he had killed Gopak stone-dead and buried him.

The blackness of the moment was lightened by Gopak. In thin, flat tones he asked, 'May I sit down? I'm tired.' He sat down, and said: 'So tired. So tired.'

Nameless still held the table. He whispered: 'Gopak...
Gopak... But I—I *killed* you. I killed you in the jungle. You
were dead. I know you were.'

Gopak passed his hand across his face. He seemed about
to cry. 'I know you did. I know. That's all I can remember—
about this earth. You killed me.' The voice became thinner and
flatter. 'And I was so comfortable. So comfortable. It was—such
a rest. Such a rest as you don't know. And then they came
and—disturbed me. They woke me up. And brought me back.'
He sat with shoulders sagged, arms drooping, hands hanging
between knees. After the first recognition, he did not look at
Nameless; he looked at the floor.

'Came and disturbed you?' Nameless leaned forward and
whispered the words. 'Woke you up? Who?'

'The Leopard Men.'

'The what?'

'The Leopard Men.' The watery voice said it as casually as
if it were saying 'the night watchman'.

'The Leopard Men?' Nameless stared, and his fat face
crinkled in an effort to take in the situation of a midnight
visitation from a dead man, and the dead man talking nonsense.
He felt his blood moving out of its course. He looked at his own
hand to see if it was his own hand. He looked at the table to
see if it was his table. The hand and the table were facts, and
if the dead man was a fact—and he was—his story might be a
fact. It seemed anyway as sensible as the dead man's presence.
He gave a heavy sigh from the stomach.

'A-ah... The Leopard Men... Yes, I heard about them out
there. Tales!'

Gopak slowly wagged his head. 'Not tales. They're real. If

they weren't real—I wouldn't be here. Would I? I'd be at rest.'

Nameless had to admit this. He had heard many tales 'out there' about the Leopard Men, and had dismissed them as jungle yarns. But now, it seemed, jungle yarns had become commonplace fact in a little London shop.

The watery voice went on. 'They do it. I saw them. I came back in the middle of a circle of them. They killed a nigger to put his life into me. They wanted a white man—for their farm. So, they brought me back. You may not believe it. You wouldn't *want* to believe it. You wouldn't want to—see or know anything like them. And I wouldn't want any man to. But it's true. That's how I'm here.'

'But I left you absolutely dead. I made every test. It was three days before I buried you. And I buried you deep.'

'I know. But that wouldn't make any difference to them. It was a long time after when they came and brought me back. And I'm still dead, you know. It's only my body they brought back.' The voice trailed into a thread, 'And I'm so tired. So tired. I want to go back—to rest.'

Sitting in his prosperous eating-house, Nameless was in the presence of an achieved miracle, but the everyday, solid appointments of the eating-house wouldn't let him fully comprehend it. Foolishly, as he realized when he had spoken, he asked Gopak to explain what had happened. Asked a man who couldn't really be alive to explain how he came to be alive. It was like asking Nothing to explain Everything.

Constantly, as he talked, he felt his grasp on his own mind slipping. The surprise of a sudden visitor at a late hour; the shock of the arrival of a long-dead man; and the realization that this long-dead man was not a wraith, were too much for him.

During the next half-hour, he found himself talking to

Gopak as to the Gopak he had known seventeen years ago
when they were partners. Then he would be halted by the
freezing knowledge that he was talking to a dead man, and that
a dead man was faintly answering him. He felt that the thing
couldn't really have happened, but in the interchange of talk
he kept forgetting the improbable side of it, and accepting it.
With each recollection of the truth, his mind would clear and
settle in one thought 'I've got to get rid of him. How am I
going to get rid of him?'

'But how did you get here?'

'I escaped.' The words came slowly and thinly, and out of
the body rather than the mouth.

'How?'

'I don't—know. I don't remember anything—except our
quarrel. And being at rest.'

'But why come all the way here? Why didn't you stay on
the coast?'

'I don't—know. But you're the only man I know. The only
man I can remember.'

'But how did you find me?'

'I don't know. But I had to—find you. You're the only man—
who can help me.'

'But how can I help you?'

The head turned weakly from side to side. 'I don't—know.
But nobody else—can.'

Nameless stared through the window, looking on to the
lamplit street and seeing nothing of it. The everyday being
which had been his half an hour ago had been annihilated; the
everyday beliefs and disbeliefs shattered and mixed together. But
some shred of his old sense and his old standard remained. He
must handle this situation. 'Well—what you want to do? What

you going to do? I don't see how I can help you. And you can't stay here, obviously.' A demon of perversity sent a facetious notion into his head—introducing Gopak to his wife—'This is my dead friend.'

But on his last spoken remark Gopak made the effort of raising his head and staring with the glazed eyes at Nameless. 'But I *must* stay here. There's nowhere else I can stay. I must stay here. That's why I came. You got to help me.'

'But you can't stay here. I got no room. All occupied. Nowhere for you to sleep.'

The wan voice said: 'That doesn't matter. I *don't* sleep.'

'Eh?'

'I *don't* sleep. I haven't slept since they brought me back. I can sit here—till you can think of some way of helping me.'

'But how *can* I?'

He again forgot the background of the situation, and began to get angry at the vision of a dead man sitting about the place waiting for him to think of something. 'How *can* I if you don't tell me how?'

'I don't—know. But you got to. *You* killed me. And I was dead—and comfortable. As it all came from you—killing me— you're responsible for me being—like this. So, you got to—help me. That's why I—came to you.'

'But what do you want me to do?'

'I don't—know. I can't—think. But nobody but you can help me. I had to come to you. Something brought me—straight to you. That means that you're the one—that can help me. Now I'm with you, something will—happen to help me. I feel it will. In time you'll—think of something.'

Nameless found his legs suddenly weak. He sat down and stared with a sick scowl at the hideous and the incomprehensible.

Here was a dead man in his house—a man he had murdered in a moment of black temper—and he knew in his heart that he couldn't turn the man out. For one thing, he would have been afraid to touch him; he couldn't see himself touching him. For another, faced with the miracle of the presence of a fifteen-years-dead man, he doubted whether physical force or any material agency would be effectual in moving the man.

His soul shivered, as all men's souls shiver at the demonstration of forces outside their mental or spiritual horizon. He had murdered this man, and often, in fifteen years, he had repented the act. If the man's appalling story were true, then he had some sort of right to turn to Nameless. Nameless recognized that, and knew that whatever happened he couldn't turn him out. His hot-tempered sin had literally come home to him.

The wan voice broke into his nightmare. 'You go to rest Nameless. I'll sit here. You go to rest.' He put his face down to his hands and uttered a little moan. 'Oh, why can't I rest? Why can't I go back to my beautiful rest?'

Nameless came down early next morning with a half-hope that Gopak would not be there. But he was there, seated where Nameless had left him last night. Nameless made some tea, and showed him where he might wash. He washed listlessly, and crawled back to his seat, and listlessly drank the tea which Nameless brought to him.

To his wife and the kitchen helpers Nameless mentioned him as an old friend who had had a bit of a shock. 'Shipwrecked and knocked on the head. But quite harmless, and he won't be staying long. He's waiting for admission to a home. A good pal to me in the past, and it's the least I can do to let him stay here a few days. Suffers from sleeplessness and prefers to sit up at night. Quite harmless.'

But Gopak stayed more than a few days. He outstayed everybody. Even when the customers had gone, Gopak was still there.

On the first morning of his visit when the regular customers came in at midday, they looked at the odd, white figure sitting vacantly in the first pew, then stared, then moved away.

All avoided the pew in which he sat. Nameless explained him to them, but his explanation did not seem to relieve the slight tension which settled on the dining-room. The atmosphere was not so brisk and chatty as usual. Even those who had their backs to the stranger seemed to be affected by his presence.

At the end of the first day, Nameless, noticing this, told him that he had arranged a nice corner of the front room upstairs, where he could sit by the window, and took his arm to take him upstairs. But Gopak feebly shook the hand away, and sat where he was. 'No. I don't want to go. I'll stay here. I'll stay here. I don't want to move.'

And he wouldn't move. After a few more pleadings Nameless realized with dismay that his refusal was definite; that it would be futile to press him or force him; that he was going to sit in that dining-room forever. He was as weak as a child and as firm as a rock.

He continued to sit in that first pew, and the customers continued to avoid it, and to give queer glances at it. It seemed that they half-recognized that he was something more than a fellow who had had a shock.

During the second week of his stay, three of the regular customers were missing, and more than one of those that remained made acidly facetious suggestions to Nameless that he park his lively friend somewhere else. He made things too exciting for them; all that whoopee took them off their work, and interfered with digestion. Nameless told them he would be staying only a day or so longer, but they found that this was untrue, and at the end of the second week, eight of the regulars had found another place.

Each day, when the dinner-hour came, Nameless tried to get him to take a little walk, but he always refused.

He would go out only at night, and then never more than two hundred yards from the shop. For the rest, he sat in his pew sometimes dozing in the afternoon, at other times staring at the floor. He took his food abstractedly, and never knew whether he had had food or not. He spoke only when questioned, and the burden of his talk was 'I'm so tired. So tired.'

One thing only seemed to arouse any light of interest in him—one thing only drew his eyes from the floor. That was the seventeen-year-old daughter of his host, who was known as Bubbles, and who helped with the waiting. And Bubbles seemed to be the only member of the shop and its customers, who did not shrink from him.

She knew nothing of the truth about him, but she seemed to understand him, and the only response he ever gave to anything was to her childish sympathy. She sat and chatted foolish chatter to him—'bringing him out of himself' she called it—and sometimes he would be brought out to the extent of a watery smile. He came to recognize her step, and would look up before she entered the room. Once or twice in the evening, when the shop was empty, and Nameless was sitting miserably with him, he would ask, without lifting his eyes. 'Where's Bubbles?' and would be told that Bubbles had gone to the pictures or was out at a dance, and would relapse into deeper vacancy. Nameless didn't like this. He was already visited by a curse which, in four weeks, had destroyed most of his business. Regular customers had dropped off two by two, and no new customers came to take their place. Strangers who dropped in once for a meal did not come again; they could not keep their eyes or their minds off the forbidding, white-faced figure sitting motionless in the first pew. At midday, when the place had been crowded and latecomers had to wait for a seat, it was now two-thirds empty; only a few of the most thick-skinned remained faithful.

And on top of this there was the interest of the dead man in his daughter, an interest which seemed to be having an unpleasant effect. Nameless hadn't noticed it, but his wife had. 'Bubbles don't seem as bright and lively as she was. You noticed it lately? She's getting quiet—and a bit slack. Sits about a lot. Paler than she used to be.'

'Her age, perhaps.'

'No, she's not one of these thin, dark sort. No—it's something else. Just the last week or two I've noticed it. Off her food. Sits about doing nothing. No interest. May be nothing; just out of sorts, perhaps... How much longer's that horrible friend of yours going to stay?'

The horrible friend stayed some weeks longer—ten weeks in all—while Nameless watched his business drop to nothing and his daughter get pale and peevish. He knew the cause of it. There was no home in all England like his: no home that had a dead man sitting in it for ten weeks. A dead man brought, after a long time, from the grave, to sit and disturb his customers and take the vitality from his daughter. He couldn't tell this to anybody. Nobody would believe such nonsense.

But he *knew* that he was entertaining a dead man, and, knowing that a long-dead man was walking the earth, he could believe in any result of that fact. He could believe almost anything that he would have derided ten weeks ago.

His customers had abandoned his shop, not because of the presence of a silent, white-faced man but because of the presence of a dead-living man.

Their minds might not know it, but their blood knew it. And as his business had been destroyed, so, he believed, would his daughter be destroyed. Her blood was not warming her; her blood told her only that this was a long-ago friend of her father's, and she was drawn to him.

It was at *this* point that Nameless, having no work to do, began to drink. And it was well that he did so. For out of the drink came an idea, and with drat idea he freed himself from the curse upon him and his house.

The shop now served scarcely half a dozen customers at midday. It had become ill-kempt and dusty, and the service and the food were bad. Nameless took no trouble to be civil to his few customers. Often, when he was notably under drink, he went to the trouble of being very rude to them. They talked about this. They talked about the decline of his business and the dustiness of the shop and the bad food. They talked about his drinking, and, of course, exaggerated it.

And they talked about the queer fellow who sat there day after day and gave everybody the creeps. A few outsiders, hearing the gossip, came to the dining-rooms to see the queer fellow and the always-tight proprietor; but they did not come again, and there were not enough of the curious to keep the place busy. It went down until it served scarcely two customers a day. And Nameless went down with it into drink.

Then, one evening, out of the drink he fished an inspiration.

He took it downstairs to Gopak, who was sitting in his usual seat, hands hanging, eyes on the floor. 'Gopak—listen. You came here because I was the only man who could help you in your trouble. You listening?'

A faint 'Yes' was his answer.

'Well, now. You told me I'd got to think of something. I've thought of something... Listen. You say I'm responsible for your condition and got to get you out of it, because I killed you. I did. We had a row. *You* made me wild. You dared me. And what with that sun and the jungle and the insects, I wasn't meself I killed you. The moment it was done I could 'a cut me right hand off. Because you and me were pals. I could 'a cut me right hand off.

'I know. I felt that directly it was over. I knew you were suffering.'

'Ah!... I have suffered. And I'm suffering now.'

'Well, this is what I've thought. All your present trouble comes from me killing you in that jungle and burying you. An idea came to me. Do you think it would help you—do you think it would put you back to rest if I—if I—if I—killed you again?'

For some seconds Gopak continued to stare at the floor. Then his shoulders moved. Then, while Nameless watched every little response to his idea, the watery voice began. 'Yes. Yes. That's it. That's what I was waiting for. That's why I came here. I can see now. That's why I had to get here. Nobody else could kill me. Only you. I've got to be lolled again. Yes, I see. But nobody else—would be able—to kill me. Only the man who first killed me... Yes, you've found—what we're both—waiting for. Anybody else could shoot me—stab me—hang me—but they couldn't kill me. Only you. That's why I managed to get here and find you.'

The watery voice rose to a thin strength. 'That's it. And you must do it. Do it now. You don't want to, I know. But you must. You *must!*'

His head dropped and he stared at the floor. Nameless, too

stared at the floor. He was seeing things. He had murdered a man and had escaped all punishment save that of his own mind, which had been terrible enough. But now he was going to murder him again—not in a jungle but in a city; and he saw the slow points of the result.

He saw the arrest. He saw the first hearing. He saw the trial. He saw the cell. He saw the rope. He shuddered.

Then he saw the alternative—the breakdown of his life—a ruined business, poverty, the poorhouse, a daughter robbed of her health and perhaps dying, and always the curse of the dead-living man, who might follow him to the poorhouse. Better to end it all he thought. Rid himself of the curse which Gopak had brought upon him and his family, and then rid his family of himself with a revolver. Better to follow up his idea.

He got stiffly to his feet. The hour was late evening—half-past ten—and the streets were quiet. He had pulled down the shop-blinds and locked the door. The room was lit by one light at the further end.

He moved about uncertainly and looked at Gopak. 'Er— how would you—how shall I—'

Gopak said, 'You did it with a knife. Just under the heart. You must do it that way again.'

Nameless stood and looked at him for some seconds. Then, with an air of resolve, he shook himself. He walked quickly to the kitchen.

Three minutes later, his wife and daughter heard a crash, as though a table had been overturned. They called but got no answer. When they came down they found him sitting in one of the pews, piping sweat from his forehead. He was white and shaking, and appeared to be recovering from a faint.

'Whatever's the matter? You all right?'

He waved them away. 'Yes, I'm all right. Touch of giddiness. Smoking too much, I think.'

'Mmmm. Or drinking—Where's your friend? Out for a walk?'

'No. He's gone off. Said he wouldn't impose any longer, and he'd go and find an infirmary.' He spoke weakly and found trouble in picking words. 'Didn't you hear that bang—when he shut the door?'

'I thought that was you fell down.'

'No. It was him when he went. I couldn't stop him.'

'Mmmm. Just as well, I think.' She looked about her. 'Things seem to 'a gone wrong since he's been here.'

There was a general air of dustiness about the place. The tablecloths were dirty, not from use but from disuse. The windows were dim. A long knife, very dusty, was lying on the table under the window. In a corner by the door leading to the kitchen, unseen by her, lay a dusty mackintosh and dungaree, which appeared to have been tossed there. But it was over by the main door, near the first pew, that the dust was thickest—a long trail of it—greyish-white dust.

'Reely this place gets more and more slapdash. Why can't you attend to business? You didn't use to be like this. No wonder it's gone down, letting the place get into this state. Why don't you pull yourself together. Just *look* at that dust by the door. Looks as though somebody's been spilling ashes all over the place.'

Nameless looked at it, and his hands shook a little. But he answered, more firmly than before: 'Yes, I know. I'll have a proper clean-up tomorrow. I'll put it all to rights tomorrow. I been getting a bit slack.'

For the first time in ten weeks he smiled at them; a thin haggard smile, but a smile.

THE WHITE WOLF OF THE HARTZ MOUNTAINS

Frederick Marryat

Before noon Philip and Krantz had embarked, and made sail in the peroqua.

They had no difficulty in steering their course; the islands by day, and the clear stars by night, were their compass. It is true that they did not follow the more direct track, but they followed the more secure, working up the smooth waters, and gaining to the northward more than to the west. Many times they were chased by the Malay proas, which infested the islands, but the swiftness of their little peroqua was their security; indeed, the chase was, generally speaking, abandoned as soon as the smallness of the vessel was made out by the pirates, who expected that little or no booty was to be gained.

One morning, as they were sailing between the isles, with less wind than usual, Philip observed—

'Krantz, you said that there were events in your own life, or connected with it, which would corroborate the mysterious tale I confided to you. Will you now tell me to what you referred?'

'Certainly,' replied Krantz; 'I have often thought of doing so, but one circumstance or another has hitherto prevented me; this is, however, a fitting opportunity. Prepare therefore to listen to a strange story, quite as strange, perhaps, as your own.

'I take it for granted that you have heard people speak of the Hartz Mountains,' observed Krantz.

'I have never heard people speak of them, that I can recollect,' replied Philip; 'but I have read of them in some book, and of the strange things which have occurred there.'

'It is indeed a wild region,' rejoined Krantz, 'and many strange tales are told of it; but strange as they are, I have good reason for believing them to be true.

'My father was not born, or originally a resident, in the Hartz Mountains; he was a serf of a Hungarian nobleman, of great possessions, in Transylvania; but although a serf, he was not by any means a poor or illiterate man. In fact, he was rich and his intelligence and respectability were such that he had been raised by his lord to the stewardship; but whoever may happen to be born a serf, a serf must he remain, even though he become a wealthy man: such was the condition of my father. My father had been married for about five years; and by his marriage had three children—my eldest brother Caesar, myself (Hermann), and a sister named Marcella. You know, Philip, that Latin is still the language spoken in that country; and that will account for our high-sounding names. My mother was a very beautiful woman, unfortunately more beautiful than virtuous: she was seen and admired by the lord of the soil; my father was sent away upon some mission; and during his absence, my mother, flattered by the attentions, and won by the assiduities of this nobleman, yielded to his wishes. It so happened that my father returned very unexpectedly, and discovered the intrigue. The evidence of my mother's shame was positive: he surprised her in the company of her seducer! Carried away by the impetuosity of his feelings, he watched the opportunity of a meeting taking place between them, and murdered both his wife and her seducer. Conscious that, as a serf, not even the provocation which he had received would be allowed as a justification of his conduct, he hastily collected together what money he could lay his hands upon, and, as we were then in the depth of winter, he put his horses to the sleigh, and taking his children with him, he set off in the middle of the night, and was far away before the tragical circumstance had transpired. Aware that he would be pursued, and that he had no chance of escape if he remained in any portion of his native country (in which the authorities could lay hold of him), he continued his flight without intermission until he had buried himself in the intricacies and seclusions of the Hartz Mountains. Of course, all that I have now told you I learned afterwards. My oldest recollections are knit to a rude, yet comfortable, cottage in which I lived with my father, brother and sister. It was on the confines of one of those vast forests which cover the northern part of Germany; around it were a few acres of ground, which, during the summer months, my father cultivated, and which, though they yielded a doubtful harvest, were sufficient for our support. In the winter we remained much indoors, for, as my father followed the chase, we were left alone, and the wolves during that season incessantly prowled about. My father had purchased the cottage, and land about it, off one of the rude foresters, who gain their livelihood partly by hunting and partly by burning charcoal, for the purpose of smelting the ore from the neighbouring mines; it was distant about two miles from any other habitation. I can call to mind the whole landscape now; the tall pines which rose up on the mountain above us, and the wide expanse of the forest beneath, on the topmost boughs and heads of whose trees we looked down from our cottage, as the mountain below us rapidly descended into the distant valley. In summer time, the prospect was beautiful; but during the severe winter, a more desolate scene could not well be imagined.

'I said that, in the winter, my father occupied himself with the chase; every day he left us, and often would he lock the door, that we might not leave the cottage. He had no one to assist him, or to take care of us—indeed, it was not easy to find a female servant who would live in such a solitude; but, could he have found one, my father would not have received her, for he had imbibed a horror of the sex, as the difference of his conduct towards us, his two boys, and my poor little sister Marcella, evidently proved. You may suppose we were sadly neglected; indeed, we suffered much, for my father, fearful that we might come to some harm, would not allow us fuel when he left the cottage; and we were obliged, therefore, to creep under the heaps of bears' skins, and there to keep ourselves as warm as we could until he returned in the evening, when a blazing fire was our delight. That my father chose this restless sort of life may appear strange, but the fact was that he could not remain quiet; whether from the remorse for having committed murder, or from the misery consequent on his change of situation, or from both combined, he was never happy unless he was in a state of activity. Children, however, when left so much to themselves, acquire a thoughtfulness not common to their age. So it was with us; and during the short cold days of winter, we would sit silent, longing for the happy hours when the snow would melt and the leaves burst out, and the birds begin their songs, and when we should again be set at liberty.

'Such was our peculiar and savage sort of life until my

brother Caesar was nine, myself seven, and my sister five years old, when the circumstances occurred on which is based the extraordinary narrative which I am about to relate.

'One evening my father returned home rather later than usual; he had been unsuccessful, and as the weather was very severe, and many feet of snow were upon the ground, he was not only very cold, but in a very bad humour. He had brought in wood, and we were all three gladly assisting each other in blowing on the embers to create a blaze, when he caught poor little Marcella by the arm and threw her aside; the child fell, struck her mouth, and bled very much. My brother ran to raise her up. Accustomed to ill-usage, and afraid of my father, she did not dare cry, but looked up in his face very piteously. My father drew his stool nearer to the hearth, muttered something in abuse of women, and busied himself with the fire, which both my brother and I had deserted when our sister was so unkindly treated. A cheerful blaze was soon the result of his exertions; but we did not, as usual, crowd round it. Marcella, still bleeding, retired to a corner, and my brother and I took our seats beside her, while my father hung over the fire gloomily and alone. Such had been our position for about half an hour when the howl of a wolf, close under the window of the cottage, fell on our ears. My father started up, and seized his gun; the howl was repeated; he examined the priming, and then hastily left the cottage, shutting the door after him. We all waited (anxiously listening), for we thought that if he succeeded in shooting the wolf, he would return in a better humour; and, although he was harsh to all of us, and particularly so to our little sister, still we loved our father, and loved to see him cheerful and happy, for what else had we to look up to? And I may here observe that perhaps there never were three children who were fonder of each other; we did not, like other children, fight and dispute together; and if, by chance, any disagreement did arise, between my elder brother and me, little Marcella would run to us, and kissing us both, seal, through her entreaties, the peace between us. Marcella was a lovely, amiable child; I can recall her beautiful features even now. Alas! Poor little Marcella.'

'She is dead, then?' observed Philip.

'Dead! Yes, dead! But how did she die? But I must not anticipate, Philip; let me tell my story.'

'We waited for some time, but the report of the gun did not reach us, and my elder brother then said, 'Our father has followed the wolf, and will not be back for some time. Marcella, let us wash the blood from your mouth, and then we will leave this corner and go to the fire to warm ourselves.'

'We did so, and remained there until near midnight, every minute wondering, as it grew later, why our father did not return. We had no idea that he was in any danger, but we thought that he must have chased the wolf for a very long time. "I will look out and see if father is coming," said my brother Caesar, going to the door. "Take care," said Marcella, "the wolves must be about now, and we cannot kill them, brother." My brother opened the door very cautiously, and but a few inches; he peeped out. "I see nothing," said he, after a time, and once more he joined us at the fire. "We have had no supper," said I, for my father usually cooked the meat as soon as he came home; and during his absence we had nothing but the fragments of the preceding day.

"'And if our father comes home, after his hunt, Caesar," said Marcella, "he will be pleased to have some supper; let us cook it for him and for ourselves." Caesar climbed upon the stool, and reached down some meat—I forget now whether it was venison or bear's meat, but we cut off the usual quantity, and proceeded to dress it, as we used to do under our father's superintendence. We were all busy putting it into the platters before the fire, to await his coming, when we heard the sound of a horn. We listened—there was a noise outside, and a minute afterwards my father entered, ushered in a young female and a large dark man in a hunter's dress.

'Perhaps I had better now relate what was only known to me many years afterwards. When my father had left the cottage, he perceived a large white wolf about thirty yards from him; as soon as the animal saw my father, it retreated slowly, growling and snarling. My father followed; the animal did not run, but always kept at some distance; and my father did not like to fire until he was pretty certain that his ball would take effect; thus they went on for some time, the wolf now leaving my father far behind, and then stopping and snarling defiance at him, and then, again, on his approach, setting off at speed.

'Anxious to shoot the animal (for the white wolf is very rare), my father continued the pursuit for several hours, during which he continually ascended the mountain.

'You must know, Philip, that there are peculiar spots on those mountains which are supposed, and, as my story will prove, truly supposed, to be inhabited by the evil influences: they are well known to the huntsmen, who invariably avoid them. Now, one of these spots, an open space in the pine forest above us, had been pointed out to my father as dangerous on that account. But whether he disbelieved these wild stories, or whether, in his eager pursuit of the chase, he disregarded them, I know not; certain, however, it is, that he was decoyed by the white wolf to his open space, when the animal appeared to slacken her speed. My father approached, came close up to her, raised his gun to his shoulder and was about to fire, when the wolf suddenly disappeared. He thought that the snow on the ground must have dazzled his sight, and he let down his gun to look for the beast—but she was gone; how she could have escaped over the clearance, without him seeing her, was beyond his comprehension. Mortified at the ill-success of his chase, he was about to retrace his steps, when he heard the distant sound of a horn. Astonishment at such a sound—at such an hour—in such a wilderness made him forget for the moment his disappointment, and he remained riveted to the spot. In a minute the horn was blown a second time, and at no great distance; my father stood still, and listened; a third time it was blown. I forget the term used to express it, but it was the signal which, my father well knew, implied that the party was lost in the woods. In a few minutes more, my father beheld a man on horseback, with a female seated on the crupper, enter the cleared space, and ride up to him. At first, my father called to mind the strange stories which he had heard of the supernatural beings who were said to frequent these mountains; but the nearer approach of the parties satisfied him that they were mortals like himself. As soon as they came up to him, the man who guided the horse accosted him, "Friend hunter, you are out late, the better fortune for us; we have ridden far, and are in fear of our lives, which are eagerly sought after. These mountains have enabled us to elude our pursuers; but if we find not shelter and refreshment, that will avail us little, as we must perish from hunger and the inclemency of the night. My daughter, who rides behind me, is now more dead than alive—say, can you assist us in our difficulty?"

"'My cottage is some few miles distant," replied my father, "but I have little to offer you besides a shelter from the weather;

to the little I have you are welcome. May I ask whence you come?"

"'Yes, friend, it is no secret now; we have escaped from Transylvania, where my daughter's honour and my life were equally in jeopardy!"

'This information was quite enough to raise an interest in my father's heart. He remembered his own escape: he remembered the loss of his wifc's honour, and the tragedy by which it was wound up. He immediately, and warmly, offered all the assistance which he could afford them.

"'There is no time to be lost, then, good sir," observed the horseman; "my daughter is chilled with the frost, and cannot hold out much longer against the severity of the weather."

"'Follow me," replied my father, leading the way towards his home.

"'I was lured away in pursuit of a large white wolf," observed my father; "it came to the very window of my hut, or I should not have been out at this time of night."

"'The creature passed by us just as we came out of the wood," said the female, in a silvery tone.

"'I was nearly discharging my piece at it," observed the hunter; "but since it did us such good service, I am glad that I allowed it to escape."

'In about an hour and a half, during which my father walked at a rapid pace, the party arrived at the cottage, and, as I said before, came in.

"'We are in good time, apparently," observed the dark hunter, catching the smell of the roasted meat, as he walked to the fire and surveyed my brother and sister and myself. "You have young cooks here, Meinheer." "I am glad that we shall not have to wait," replied my father. "Come, seat yourself by the fire; you require warmth after your cold ride." "And where can I put up my horse, Meinheer?" observed the huntsman. "I will take care of him," replied my father, going out of the cottage door.

'The female must, however, be particularly described. She was young, and apparently twenty years of age. She was dressed in a travelling dress, deeply bordered with white fur, and wore a cap of white ermine on her head. Her features were very beautiful, at least I thought so, and so my father has since declared. Her hair was flaxen, glossy, and shining, and bright as a mirror; and her mouth, although somewhat large when it was open, showed the most brilliant teeth I have ever beheld. But there was something about her eyes, bright as they were, which made us children afraid; they were so restless, so furtive; I could not at that time tell why, but I felt as if there was cruelty in her eye; and when she beckoned us to come to her, we approached her with fear and trembling. Still she was beautiful, very beautiful. She spoke kindly to my brother and myself, patted our heads and caressed us; but Marcella would not come near her; on the contrary, she slunk away, and hid herself in bed, and would not wait for the supper, which half an hour before she had been so anxious for.

'My father, having put the horse into a close shed, soon returned, and supper was placed on the table. When it was over, my father requested the young lady take possession of the bed, and he would remain at the fire, and sit up with her father. After some hesitation on her part, this arrangement was agreed to, and I and my brother crept into the other bed with Marcella, for we had as yet always slept together.

'But we could not sleep; there was something so unusual, not only in seeing strange people, but in having those people sleep at the cottage, that we were bewildered. As for poor little Marcella, she was quiet, but I perceived that she trembled during the whole night, and sometimes I thought that she was checking a sob. My father had brought out some spirits, which he rarely used, and he and the strange hunter remained drinking and talking before the fire. Our ears were ready to catch the slightest whisper—so much was our curiosity excited.

"'You said you came from Transylvania?' observed my father.

"'Even so, Meinheer,' replied the hunter. 'I was a serf to the noble house; my master would insist upon my surrendering up my fair girl to his wishes; it ended in my giving him a few inches of my hunting-knife.'

"'We are countrymen and brothers in misfortune,' replied my father, taking the huntsman's hand and pressing it warmly.

"'Indeed! Are you then from that country?'

"'Yes; and I too have fled for my life. But mine is a melancholy tale.'

"'Your name?' inquired the hunter.

"'Krantz.'

"'What! I have heard your tale; you need not renew your grief by repeating it now. Welcome, most welcome, Meinheer, and, I may say, my worthy kinsman. I am your second cousin, Wilfred of Barnsdorf,' cried the hunter, raising up and embracing my father.

'They filled their horn-mugs to the brim, and drank to one another after the German fashion. The conversation was then carried on in a low tone; all that we could collect from it was that our new relative and his daughter were to take up their abode in our cottage, at least for the present. In about an hour, they both fell back in their chairs and appeared to sleep.

'"Marcella, dear, did you hear?" said my brother, in a low tone.

'"Yes," replied Marcella, in a whisper, "I heard all. Oh! brother, I cannot bear to look upon that woman—I feel so frightened."

'My brother made no reply, and shortly afterwards we were all three fast asleep.

'When we awoke the next morning, we found that the hunter's daughter had risen before us. I thought she looked more beautiful than ever. She came up to little Marcella and caressed her; the child burst into tears, and sobbed as if her heart would break.

'But not to detain you with too long a story, the huntsman and his daughter were accommodated in the cottage. My father and he went out hunting daily, leaving Christina with us. She performed all the household duties; was very kind to us children; and gradually the dislike even of little Marcella wore away. But a great change took place in my father; he appeared to have conquered his aversion to the sex, and was most attentive to Christina. Often, after her father and we were in bed, would he sit up with her, conversing in a low tone by the fire. I ought to have mentioned that my father and the huntsman Wilfred slept in another portion of the cottage, and that the bed which he formerly occupied, and which was in the same room as ours, had been given up to the use of Christina. These visitors had been about three weeks at the cottage, when, one night, after we children had been sent to bed, a consultation was held. My father had asked Christina in marriage, and had obtained both her own consent and that of Wilfred; after this, a conversation took place, which was, as nearly as I can recollect, as follows—

'"You may take my child, Meinheer Krantz, and my blessing

with her, and I shall then leave you and seek some other habitation—it matters little where."

"'Why not remain here, Wilfred?'"

"'No, no, I am called elsewhere; let that suffice, and ask no more questions. You have my child.'"

"'I thank you for her, and will duly value her but there is one difficulty.'"

"'I know what you would say; there is no priest here in this wild country; true; neither is there any law to bind. Still must some ceremony pass between you, to satisfy a father. Will you consent to marry her after my fashion? If so, I will marry you directly.'"

"'I will,' replied my father."

"'Then take her by the hand. Now, Meinheer, swear.'"

"'I swear,' repeated my father."

"'By all the spirits of the Hartz Mountains—'"

"'Nay, why not by Heaven?' interrupted my father."

"'Because it is not my humour,' rejoined Wilfred. "If I prefer that oath, less binding, perhaps, than another, surely you will not thwart me.'"

"'Well, be it so, then; have your humour. Will you make me swear by that in which I do not believe?'"

"'Yet many do so, who in outward appearance are Christians,' rejoined Wilfred; "say, will you be married, or shall I take my daughter away with me?'

"'Proceed,' replied my father impatiently."

"'I swear by all the spirits of the Hartz Mountains, by all their power for good or for evil, that I take Christina for my wedded wife; that I will ever protect her, cherish her, and love her; that my hand shall never be raised against her to harm her.'"

'My father repeated the words after Wilfred.

"'And if I fail in this my vow, may all the vengeance of the spirits fall upon me and upon my children; may they perish by the vulture, by the wolf, or other beasts of the forest; may their flesh be torn from their limbs, and their bones blanch in the wilderness: all this I swear."

My father hesitated, as he repeated the last words; little Marcella could not restrain herself, and as my father repeated the last sentence, she burst into tears. This sudden interruption appeared to discompose the party, particularly my father; he spoke harshly to the child, who controlled her sobs, burying her face under the bedclothes.

'Such was the second marriage of my father. The next morning, the hunter Wilfred mounted his horse and rode away.

'My father resumed his bed, which was in the same room as ours; and things went on much as before the marriage, except that our new stepmother did not show any kindness towards us; indeed, during my father's absence, she would often beat us, particularly little Marcella, and her eyes would flash fire, as she looked eagerly upon the fair and lovely child.

'One night my sister awoke me and my brother.

"'What is the matter?" asked Caesar.

"'She has gone out," whispered Marcella.

"'Gone out!"

"'Yes, gone out at the door, in her nightclothes," replied the child; "I saw her get out of bed, look at my father to see if he slept, and then she went out the door."

'What could induce her to leave her bed, and all undressed to go out, in such bitter wintry weather, with the snow deep on the ground, was to us incomprehensible; we lay awake, and in about an hour we heard the growl of a wolf close under the window.

'"There is a wolf," said Caesar. "She will be torn to pieces."

'"Oh, no!" cried Marcella.

'In a few minutes our stepmother appeared; she was in her nightdress, as Marcella had stated. She let down the latch of the door, so as to make no noise, went to a pail of water, and washed her face and hands, and then slipped into the bed where my father lay.

'We all three trembled—we hardly knew why; but we resolved to watch the next night. We did so; and not only on the ensuing night, but on many others, and always at about the same hour would our stepmother rise from her bed and leave the cottage; and after she was gone, we invariably heard the growl of a wolf under our window, and always saw her on her return wash herself before she retired to bed. We observed also that she seldom sat down to meals, and that when she did she appeared to eat with dislike; but when the meat was taken down to be prepared for dinner, she would often furtively put a raw piece into her mouth.

'My brother Caesar was a courageous boy; he did not like to speak to my father until he knew more. He resolved that he would follow her out, and ascertain what she did. Marcella and I endeavoured to dissuade him from the project; but he would not be controlled; and the very next night, he lay down in his clothes, and as soon as our stepmother had left the cottage he jumped up, took down my father's gun, and followed her.

'You may imagine in what a state of suspense Marcella and I remained during his absence. After a few minutes we heard the report of a gun. It did not awaken my father; and we lay trembling with anxiety. In a minute afterwards we saw our stepmother enter the cottage—her dress was bloody. I put my hand to Marcella's mouth to prevent her crying out, although I was myself in great alarm. Our stepmother approached my father's bed, looked to see if he was asleep, and then went to the chimney and blew up the embers into a blaze.

"'Who is there?" asked my father, waking up.

"'Lie still, dearest," replied my stepmother; "it is only me; I have lighted the fire to warm some water; I am not quite well."

'My father turned round, and was soon asleep; but we watched our stepmother. She changed her linen, and threw the garments she had worn into the fire; and we then perceived that her right leg was bleeding profusely, as if from a gunshot wound. She bandaged it up, and then dressing herself remained before the fire until the break of day.

'Poor little Marcella, her heart beat quick as she pressed me to her side—so indeed did mine. Where was our brother Caesar? How did my stepmother receive the wound unless from his gun? At last my father rose, and then for the first time I spoke, saying, "Father, where is my brother Caesar?"

"'Your brother?" exclaimed he; "why, where can he be?"

"'Merciful Heaven! I thought as I lay very restless last night," observed our stepmother, "that I heard somebody open the latch of the door; and, dear me, husband, what has become of your gun?"

'My father cast his eyes up above the chimney, and perceived that his gun was missing and for a moment he looked perplexed; then, seizing a broad axe, he went out of the cottage without saying another world.

'He did not remain away from us long; in a few minutes he returned, bearing in his arms the mangled body of my poor brother; he laid it down, and covered up his face.

'My stepmother rose up, and looked at the body, while

Marcella and I threw ourselves by its side, wailing and sobbing bitterly.

'"Go to bed again, children," said she sharply. "Husband," continued she, "your boy must have taken the gun down to shoot a wolf, and the animal has been too powerful for him. Poor boy! He has paid dearly for his rashness."

'My father made no reply. I wished to speak—to tell all—but Marcella, who perceived my intention, held me by the arm, and looked at me so imploringly, that I desisted.

'My father, therefore, was left in his error; but Marcella and I, although we could not comprehend it, were conscious that our stepmother was in some way connected with my brother's death.

'That day my father went out and dug a grave; and when he laid the body in the earth he piled up stones over it, so that the wolved should not be able to dig it up. The shock of this catastrophe was to my poor father very severe; for several days he never went to the chase, although at times he would utter bitter anathemas and vengeance against the wolves.

'But during this time of mourning on his part, my stepmother's nocturnal wanderings continued with the same regularity as before.

'At last my father took down his gun to repair to the forest; but he soon returned, and appeared much annoyed.

'"Would you believe it, Christina, that the wolves—perdition to the whole race!—have actually contrived to dig up the body of my poor boy, and now there is nothing left of him but his bones."

'"Indeed!" replied my stepmother. Marcella looked at me, and I saw in her intelligent eye all she would have uttered.

'"A wolf growls under our window every night, father," said I.

"'Ay, indeed! Why did you not tell me, boy? Wake me the next time you hear it.'"

'I saw my stepmother turn away; her eyes flashed fire, and she gnashed her teeth.

'My father went out again, and covered up with a larger pile of stones the little remains of my poor brother which the wolves had spared. Such was the first act of the tragedy.

'The spring now came on; the snow disappeared, and we were permitted to leave the cottage; but never would I quit for one moment my dear little sister, to whom, since the death of my brother, I was more ardently attached than ever; indeed, I was afraid to leave her alone with my stepmother, who appeared to have a particular pleasure in ill-treating the child. My father was now employed upon his little farm, and I was able to render him some assistance.

'Marcella used to sit by us while we were at work, leaving my stepmother alone in the cottage. I ought to observe that, as the spring advanced, so did my stepmother decrease her nocturnal rambles, and that we never heard the growl of the wolf under the window after I had spoken of it to my father.

'One day, when my father and I were in the field, Marcella being with us, my stepmother came out, saying that she was going into the forest to collect some herbs that my father wanted, and that Marcella must go to the cottage and watch the dinner. Marcella went; and my stepmother soon disappeared in the forest, taking a direction quite contrary to that in which the cottage stood, and leaving my father and me, as it were, between her and Marcella.

'About an hour afterwards we were startled by shrieks from the cottage—evidently the shrieks of little Marcella. "Marcella has burnt herself, father," said I, throwing down my spade. My father threw down his, and we both hastened to the cottage. Before we could gain the door, out darted a large white wolf, which fled with the utmost celerity. My father had no weapon; he rushed into the cottage, and there saw poor little Marcella expiring. Her body was dreadfully mangled and the blood pouring from it had formed a large pool on the cottage floor. My father's first intention had been to seize his gun and pursue; but he was checked by this horrid spectacle; he knelt down by his dying child, and burst into tears. Marcella could just look kindly on us for a few seconds, and then her eyes were closed in death.

'My father and I were still hanging over my poor sister's body when my stepmother came in. At the dreadful sight, she expressed much concern; but she did not appear to recoil from the sight of blood, as most people do.

'"Poor child!" said she, "it must have been that great white wolf which passed me just now, and frightened me so. She's quite dead, Krantz."

'"I know it!—I know it!" cried my father, in agony.

'I thought my father would never recover from the effects of this second tragedy; he mourned bitterly over the body of his sweet child, and for several days would not consign it to its grave, although frequently requested by my stepmother to do so. At last he yielded, and dug a grave for her close by that of my poor brother, and took every precaution that the wolves should not violate her remains.

'I was now really miserable as I lay alone in the bed which I had formerly shared with my brother and sister. I could not help thinking that my stepmother was implicated in both their deaths, although I could not account for the manner; but I no longer felt afraid of her; my little heart was full of hatred and revenge.

'The night after my sister had been buried, as I lay awake, I perceived my stepmother get up and go out of the cottage. I waited some time, then dressed myself, and looked out through the door, which I half opened. The moon shone bright, and I could see the spot where my brother and my sister had been buried; and what was my horror when I perceived my stepmother busily removing the stones from Marcella's grave!

'She was in her white nightdress, and the moon shone full upon her. She was digging with her hands, and throwing away the stones behind her with all the ferocity of a wild beast. It was some time before I could collect my senses and decide what I should do. At last I perceived that she had arrived at the body, and raised it up to the side of the grave. I could bear it no longer: I ran to my father and awoke him.

'"Father, father!" cried I, "dress yourself, and get your gun."

'"What!" cried my father, "the wolves are there, are they?"

'He jumped out of bed, threw on his clothes, and in his anxiety did not appear to perceive the absence of his wife. As soon as he was ready, I opened the door; he went out, and I followed him.

'Imagine his horror, when (unprepared as he was for such a sight) he beheld, as he advanced towards the grave, not a wolf, but his wife, in her nightdress, on her hands and knees, crouching by the body of my sister, and tearing off large pieces of flesh, and devouring them with all the avidity of a wolf. She was too busy to be aware of our approach. My father dropped his gun; his hair stood on end, so did mine; he breathed heavily, and then his breath for a time stopped. I picked up the gun and put it into his hand. Suddenly he appeared as if concentrated rage had restored him to double vigour; he levelled his piece, fired, and with a loud shriek down fell the wretch whom he had fostered in his bosom.

'"God of heaven!" cried my father, sinking down upon the earth in a swoon, as soon as he had discharged his gun.

'I remained some time by his side before he recovered. "Where am I?" said he, "What has happened? Oh!—yes, yes! I recollect now. Heaven forgive me!"

'He rose and we walked up to the grave; imagine our astonishment and horror to find that, instead of the dead body of my stepmother, as we expected, there was, lying over the remains of my poor sister, a large white she-wolf.

'"The white wolf," exclaimed my father, "the white wolf which decoyed me into the forest—I see it all now—I have dealt with the spirits of the Hartz Mountains."

'For some time my father remained in silence and deep thought. He then carefully lifted the body of my sister, replaced it in the grave, and covered it over as before, having struck the head of the dead animal with the heel of his boot, and raving like a madman. He walked back to the cottage, shut the door, and threw himself on the bed; I did the same, for I was in a stupor of amazement.

'Early in the morning we were both roused by a loud knocking at the door, and in rushed the hunter Wilfred.

'"My daughter—man—my daughter!—where is my daughter?" cried he in a rage.

'"Where the wretch, the fiend should be, I trust," replied my father, starting up, and displaying equal choler: "where she should be—in hell! Leave this cottage, or you may fare worse."

'"Ha—ha!" replied the hunter, "would you harm a potent spirit of the Hartz Mountains? Poor mortal, who must needs wed a werewolf."

'"Out, demon! I defy thee and thy power."

'"Yet shall you feel it; remember your oath—your solemn

oath—never to raise your hand against her to harm her."

"'I made no compact with evil spirits."

"'You did, and if you failed in your vow, you were to meet the vengeance of the spirits. Your children were to perish by the vulture, the wolf—"

"'Out, out, demon!"

"'And their bones blanch in the wilderness. Ha—ha!"

'My father, frantic with rage, seized his axe and raised it over Wilfred's head to strike.

"'All this I swear," continued the huntsman mockingly.

'The axe descended; but it passed through the form of the hunter, and my father lost his balance, and fell heavily on the floor.

"'Mortal!" said the hunter, striding over my father's body, "We have power over those only who have committed murder. You have been guilty of a double murder: you shall pay the penalty attached to your marriage vow. Two of your children are gone, the third is yet to follow—and follow them he will, for your oath is registered. Go—it were kindness to kill thee—your punishment is, that you live!"

'With these words the spirit disappeared. My father rose from the floor, embraced me tenderly, and knelt down in prayer.

'The next morning he quitted the cottage for ever. He took me with him, and bent his steps to Holland, where we safely arrived. He had some little money with him; but he had not been many days in Amsterdam before he was seized with a brain fever, and died raving mad. I was put into the asylum, and afterwards was sent to sea before the mast. You now know all my history. The question is, whether I am to pay the penalty of my father's oath? I am myself perfectly convinced that, in some way or another, I shall.'

II

On the twenty-second day the high land of the south of Sumatra was in view: as there were no vessels in sight, they resolved to keep their course through the Straits, and run for Pulo Penang, which they expected, as their vessel lay so close to the wind, to reach in seven or eight days. By constant exposure Philip and Krantz were now so bronzed that with their long beards and Mussulman dresses, they might easily have passed off for natives. They had steered during the whole of the days exposed to a burning sun; they had lain down and slept in the dew of the night; but their health had not suffered. But for several days, since he had confided the history of his family to Philip, Krantz had become silent and melancholy; his usual flow of spirits had vanished, and Philip had often questioned him as to the cause. As they entered the Straits, Philip talked of what they should do upon their arrival at Goa; when Krantz gravely replied, 'For some days, Philip, I have had a presentiment that I shall never see that city.'

'You are out of health, Krantz,' replied Philip.

'No, I am in sound health, body and mind. I have endeavoured to shake off the presentiment, but in vain; there is a warning voice that continually tells me that I shall not be long with you Philip; will you oblige me by making me content on one point? I have gold about my person which may be useful to you; oblige me by taking it, and securing it on your own.'

'What nonsense, Krantz.'

'It is no nonsense, Philip. Have you not had your warnings? Why should I not have mine? You know that I have little fear in my composition, and that I care not about death; but I feel the presentiment which I speak of more strongly every hour...'

'These are the imaginings of a disturbed brain, Krantz;

why you, young, in full health and vigour, should not pass your days in peace, and live to a good old age, there is no cause for believing. You will be better tomorrow.'

'Perhaps so,' replied Krantz; 'but you still must yield to my whim, and take the gold. If I am wrong, and we do arrive safe, you know, Philip, you can let me have it back,' observed Krantz, with a faint smile—'but you forget, our water is nearly out, and we must look out for a rill on the coast to obtain a fresh supply.'

'I was thinking of that when you commenced this unwelcome topic. We had better look out for the water before dark, and as soon as we have replenished our jars, we will make sail again.'

At the time that this conversation took place, they were on the eastern side of the Strait, about forty miles to the northward. The interior of the coast was rocky and mountainous, but it slowly descended to low lands of alternate forest and jungles, which continued to the beach; the country appeared to be uninhabited. Keeping close in to the shore, they discovered, after two hours' run, a fresh stream which burst in a cascade from the mountains, and swept its devious course through the jungle, until it poured its tribute into the waters of the Strait.

They ran close into the mouth of the stream, lowered the sails, and pulled the peroqua against the current until they had advanced far enough to assure them that the water was quite fresh. The jars were soon filled, and they were again thinking of pushing off, when enticed by the beauty of the spot, the coolness of the fresh water, and wearied with their long confinement on board of the peroqua, they proposed to bathe—a luxury hardly to be appreciated by those who have not been in a similar situation. They threw off their Mussulman dresses, and plunged into the stream, where they remained for some time. Krantz was the first to get out; he complained of feeling chilled, and he walked on to the banks where their clothes had been laid. Philip also approached nearer to the beach, intending to follow him.

'And now, Philip,' said Krantz, 'this will be a good opportunity for me to give you the money. I will open my sash and pour it out, and you can put it into your own before you put it on.'

Philip was standing in the water, which was about level with his waist.

'Well, Krantz,' said he, 'I suppose if it must be so, it must; but it appears to me an idea so ridiculous—however, you shall have your own way.'

Philip quitted the run, and sat down by Krantz, who was already busy in shaking the doubloons out of the folds of his sash; at last he said—

'I believe, Philip, you have got them all, now? I feel satisfied.'

'What danger there can be to you, which I am not equally exposed to, I cannot conceive,' replied Philip: 'however—'

Hardly had he said these words, when there was a tremendous roar—a rush like a mighty wind through the air—a blow which threw him on his back—a loud cry—and a contention. Philip recovered himself, and perceived the naked form of Krantz carried off with the speed of an arrow by an enormous tiger through the jungle. He watched with distended eyeballs; in a few seconds the animal and Krantz had disappeared.

'God of Heaven! Would that Thou hadst spared me this,' cried Philip, throwing himself down in agony on his face. 'O Krantz! My friend—my brother—too sure was your presentiment. Merciful God! Have pity—but Thy will be done.' And Philip burst into a flood of tears.

For more than an hour did he remain fixed upon the spot, careless and indifferent to the danger by which he was surrounded. At last, somewhat recovered, he rose, dressed himself, and then again sat down—his eyes fixed upon the clothes of Krantz, and the gold which still lay on the sand.

'He would give me that gold. He foretold his doom. Yes! Yes! It was his destiny, and it has been fulfilled. His bones will bleach in the wilderness, and the spirit-hunter and his wolfish daughter are avenged.'

THE OLD GRAVEYARD AT SIRUR

C.A. Kincaid

When I was judge of Poona several years before the Great War, my tours of inspection used to, at times, take me to Sirur, the old cantonment some 40 miles from Poona that had housed the Poona Horse ever since the conquest of 1818. Not far from the officers' mess and their mud bungalows was the old cemetery. It was no longer used, but it contained the graves of officers of former generations who had succumbed to cholera, enteric fever and the score of other diseases that in eastern lands lie in wait for the English soldier. In the centre rose a tombstone considerably bigger than the others and I often noticed the Indian troopers salute it as they passed. I was loth to question the officers of the Poona Horse, although I knew one or two of them fairly well. It was none of my business and I thought that they might think me impertinent if I probed the matter. One day, however, after seeing several men salute very rigidly with eyes turned towards the central monument, I could no longer control my curiosity; and, meeting a Captain Johnson, an excellent and understanding gentleman, I blurted out:

'Excuse my stupid curiosity; but would you mind telling me why your troopers salute so regularly and so correctly the graveyard. Although they very rightly honour their living superiors, I find it strange that they should salute the dead as well.'

'Oh they don't salute the graveyard; they salute old Colonel Hutchings. He commanded the regiment in the 1820s. He comes out, so they say, and sits on his tomb. It is that big one in the centre. He sits on it and every now and then his wife joins him.'

'My dear chap, what are you talking about? They are both dead as doornails. Do you mean their ghosts sit on the tombstone? Have you seen them yourself?'

'Well, I don't know,' said Johnson, looking rather confused. 'I thought I did once or twice; but it was no doubt my imagination.'

'I say, do tell me: who was this Colonel Hutchings? Why does he sit on his tomb? Who was his wife? Why does she sit on his tomb, too?'

'Look here,' said Johnson good-humouredly. 'I know what an infernal prober you are; but I have neither the time nor the knowledge to stand your cross-examination. You are going into Poona shortly; send for old Rissaldar Major Shinde. I'll write you down his address. He knows all about Colonel Hutchings; he tells us the story after mess sometimes, when we ask him to come to Sirur, as we do once a year at the time of our annual regimental sports. He retired ages ago, but his memory is as fresh as ever.'

As Johnson spoke he wrote down the name of the Rissaldar Major and his address in Shukurwar Peth, a well-known quarter in Poona city.

Shortly after my return to headquarters, I sent a line from the Sangam, the judge's official residence, to Rissaldar Major Shinde. I begged him kindly to call on me at 9 a.m. any day that he might be free. I mentioned Captain Johnson's name and told him frankly that I wanted to hear all he could tell me about the cemetery at Sirur, and especially Colonel Hutchings' tomb. Two mornings later, a fine old Maratha gentleman drove up in a tonga and was shewn in with every sign of respect by the judge's macebearer.

After shaking my visitor cordially by the hand, I thanked him for coming, and said: 'Your name is Shinde, is it not? Are you a member of the family of H.H. the Maharaja of that name?'

'I, Sahib, am a Shinde of Kizarnagar; and you, who have studied our history will remember how the great Madhavrao Shinde would have given up all his titles to be one of my family; but that is another matter. I read in your letter that you wanted to hear about Colonel Hutchings Sahib. He was in a sense more nearly related to me than H.H. the Maharaja; for he married a lady of our family.'

'Married a lady of your family? What do you mean, Rissaldar Sahib? He was an Englishman and he could not have married a lady of your family. Nor would her parents have allowed her to marry a Christian no matter who he was.'

'Yes, indeed, Sahib, he did, and that was the cause of the trouble. If you care to listen, I shall tell you the story.'

'Oh, please do.'

'Colonel Hutchings Sahib, so my father used to tell me, was stationed at Kirkee before the Peshwa fought the English in 1818. Hutchings was then a handsome young Captain Sahib and was, it appears, very attractive to our women. One day, he and a squadron of horse, mostly recruited from Musulmans and Mhars and all ready to die for their English leader, were riding along the banks of the Muta Mula (River) below where the great dam and bridge now are. It so happened that one of the Shindes of Kizarnagar had died, and, as was then the custom of our family, his widow had given out that she would become a suttee and burn with her lord. She was, however, quite a young girl, probably not more than fifteen years of age. When she saw the pyre ready for her to ascend, she lost all control of herself and began to scream and struggle like a maniac. Her mother and married sister tried to soothe her and offered her opium, so that she might be drugged and not feel the pain of burning. But no, Sahib, the widow woman would not listen. One of her brothers wished to stun her with a blow from one of the logs from the pyre; but her mother was reluctant to have this done; for the women of her family—she was a Ghatle from Kolhapur—had never before flinched from the flames. She thought that it would be a disgrace if her daughter did not sit erect on the pyre with her husband's head on her lap and a candle held upright in each hand.

'Just then Hutchings Sahib rode up. The widow, seeing a foreigner, called to him for help. Hutchings Sahib was then a brave young soldier. He did not understand that he was about to insult our holy religion. All he saw was a young and pretty woman, calling to him to save her from a painful death. He turned to his squadron and said: "Well, brothers, will you help me to carry her out of danger?" Of course those Mlecchas and untouchables were only too pleased. So he charged the crowd. Unarmed, and taken by surprise, they offered little resistance. The dead man's brothers did indeed shew fight; but they were cut down and one of them killed. A couple of Mhars lifted the widow woman in front of Hutchings Sahib's saddle. He turned his horse, rallied his squadron and rode back to Kirkee. There he got a Portuguese padre Sahib, who lived with the Portuguese troops of the Peshwa's army, to marry him to the widow. Thus, when the Peshwa's minister complained to Elphinston Sahib, the resident, and demanded the woman back that she might complete the suttee ceremony, Elphinston Sahib said as she had by her second marriage become an Englishwoman and a subject of the king of England, he would not give her up.

'The Peshwa's government told our people and added that owing to the widow woman's remarriage they could do nothing for us. We were furious. The suttee ceremony had been stopped. All the merit that would thereby have been acquired by our dead relative had been lost. The widow had been carried off, our kinsmen had been killed, and we were to get no redress. Well, we resolved that if the Peshwa would not help us we should help ourselves. We vowed that we should kill Hutchings Sahib and the widow woman also.'

'You say "we", Rissaldar Sahib, but you could not have been alive then.'

'Quite true, Sahib. I was not born until many years afterwards. I am only seventy years old now. By "we" I mean the Shindes of Kizarnagar.'

'I understand; but do go on, Rissaldar Sahib, with your story.'

'As the Sahib pleases. We vowed, as I have said, to kill Hutchings Sahib. It was not, however, easy. Hutchings Sahib and the widow woman lived in a house almost surrounded by the troopers' lines; and as a rumour had spread that we sought their lives, the lines were well-guarded and no one allowed inside. One day, it is true, two of our people got through the gates, but before they could do anything they were caught, beaten half-dead and thrown out. This added fuel to our hatred; still we could do nothing, for not long afterwards the Peshwa fought the English and they beat him at Kirkee and Ashta. In the end, he surrendered and the English, as the Sahib knows, took his country. The Poona Horse were stationed at Sirur. Hutchings Sahib had fought very bravely in the war and he was promoted to command the regiment and to be a Colonel Sahib. He, of course, went to live there too and the widow woman went with him; and all the time we were eating our hearts out with ungratified hatred. It must have been six years after he had risen to command the regiment and was about to return to England that our chance came. We had long hung about Sirur in vain, for he was very cautious. One day, however, when he went a little way out of Sirur in a palki, either to shoot blackbuck or chinkara, four of our men rushed out of their hiding place in the dry bed of a river. Slashing the palki bearers' legs with our swords, we made them drop the palki and then we fell on the Colonel and killed him. His gun was unloaded, but he made a great fight and with his sword wounded two of our men before we could finish him. This was our undoing; for the palki men ran back and told the widow woman. She told the police that the murderers must have been Shindes from our village. The police went there and, finding two of our men with unhealed wounds, arrested them. They were identified by the palki bearers and hanged. We were now resolved to kill the widow at all costs; but a day or two after the execution she took opium, died and was buried besides the Colonel Sahib. The officers raised the big monument that you have seen over both of them; but they have carved on it only the name of Hutchings Sahib; for they were ashamed of his marriage to a woman not of his race. Ever since the Colonel Sahib sits from time to time on his tomb. Sometimes, although more rarely, the widow woman sits beside him; so the troopers always salute as they pass the tomb. Everyone of them has at one time or another seen him in the spirit.'

'So that is the tale, Rissaldar Sahib, thank you ever so much for it.'

'There is no need for thanks, Sahib. It is I who should thank you for your courteous hearing. Moreover, that is not all the story, there is more to tell; only no doubt the Sahib is weary and I shall come again some other day.'

'Oh no, Rissaldar Sahib,' I said quickly, afraid that I should lose the rest of the yarn. 'Do go on. So far from tiring me, your words have made me feel young again.'

'The Presence is too kind. Well then I shall continue. Many, many years afterwards we Shindes heard that the son of Colonel Hutchings Sahib's sister, a young man called Furley Sahib, had been posted to the Poona Horse. I was then a youth of twenty years and it was arranged that I should enlist as a trooper in the same regiment and, when the chance came, kill Furley Sahib. I must admit that I was not very eager to do this. The quarrel was all so old and I realized that if my plan succeeded, I should probably be hanged; and that if I failed I should have had to work and train as a soldier for nothing. I did not want to be a soldier. I wanted to stay in Kizarnagar and farm our lands. Still my father and my elder kinsmen put such pressure on me and said so many times that it would be a family disgrace if I did not avenge the honour of the Shindes, that at length I gave way. I joined the Poona Horse as a trooper and after some time I contrived to get myself appointed as an orderly to Furley Sahib. He was a fine young man and I had no feeling of dislike towards him; but I could not escape from the task laid upon me. While I was pondering how to kill him—either by arsenic in his tea or by an open attack on him—war broke out with Afghanistan. Furley Sahib immediately got himself transferred to the 2nd Bombay Cavalry and I asked him to take me with him. I was sure that in a battle I could shoot him without anyone noticing me. Furley Sahib was pleased at my request and we went together by train until we caught up the 2nd Bombay Cavalry near the frontier. I shall not weary the Sahib with a long account of what happened. The Sahib knows the history of the war better than I do. It is enough to say that the 2nd Bombay Cavalry were sent with a body of Indian infantry and the 66th English regiment under General Burrows Sahib to hold Kandahar. Stuart Sahib occupied Kabul. One day Burrows Sahib's scouts told him that Ayub Khan and some 5,000 Afghans were assembled in the hills only six or seven miles away. Burrows Sahib decided to attack Ayub Khan and disperse his force before it grew to a great army; for the Afghans were streaming to join Ayub Khan from all quarters. Next morning, Burrows Sahib and his brigade moved out against Ayub Khan; but we soon learnt that the scouts had either lied deliberately or had themselves been misled. We went more than twelve miles before we saw the Afghans and then we found that they numbered 50,000 and not 5,000. Nevertheless Burrows Sahib gave orders to attack; indeed he could hardly have done otherwise, for the enemy were advancing against him at great speed. We of the 2nd Bombay Cavalry were on the right flank and three of the squadrons were commanded by three Monteith brothers, who that day shewed themselves to be real soldiers, very brave and skilful. Suddenly we heard a buzzing noise far away to the left. This was the first rush of the Afghan Ghazis and their shouts reached us in the distance like the hum of bees swarming at the end of the Deccan cold weather. Burrows Sahib formed his infantry into squares and they shot so steadily that the Ghazis were stopped and forced to take cover. Then some minutes later, the Ghazis rallied and again charged with the same humming sound. Again Burrows Sahib formed his men in squares and broke the Ghazi rush with musketry fire. Then that accursed Ayub Khan brought up his guns from behind the hills and before our footsoldiers could deploy into open order, he fired with fury at our squares. Under cover of this fire the Ghazis again charged and our men, confused by the cannonade and with great gaps in their ranks, were not able to stop them as they had done before. Burrows Sahib ordered a retirement; but under the heavy cannon fire and the attacks of the Afghans our infantry broke and it seemed as if our entire army would be destroyed. It was then that the three Monteith brothers shewed such courage and skill. Every time the Ghazis tried to get round the infantry, we of the 2nd Bombay Cavalry charged, each squadron led by a Monteith Sahib. Thus the infantry were able to get back safe to Kandahar. It was during the cavalry fighting that I thought that my chance had come. Lifting my carbine, I took a steady aim at Furley Sahib's back. No one noticed me, as all the troopers were watching the Ghazis and our infantry; I was just about to pull the trigger when I was knocked off my horse by a most violent blow. Some vile Afghan had fired a jezail in our direction and the shot hit me in the chest, just as I was about to shoot Furley Sahib. At first he did not notice my fall, but when the retreat began he saw me on the ground and, lifting me up, put me on the saddle in front of him and so brought me alive to Kandahar. There he looked after me and I soon recovered. By doing this, Furley Sahib wiped out our quarrel, and from that time on I became his devoted friend; and no words of my kinsmen had any influence with me.'

'I suppose you were in Kandahar when Lord Roberts marched from Kabul to relieve you.'

The old Rissaldar Major drew himself up and saluted on hearing the famous soldier's name: 'Yes, indeed I was; the great

Roberts Sahib came all the way from Kabul with the speed of Hanuman himself. In the meantime, however, Ayub Khan had tried to take Kandahar by storm and had been beaten back with heavy loss. Many of the Afghans had deserted and we had killed and wounded some 10,000; so that Lord Roberts Sahib's task was easier than that of Burrows Sahib. Still he did his work thoroughly and so routed that demon of an Ayub Khan that he never fought the English again. That is my whole story.'

'Well, thank you ever so much for it; but what happened to Furley Sahib?'

'He got safely through the Afghan War; afterwards he returned to the Poona Horse and rose to command it. It was he who gave me my last promotion and made me a Rissaldar Major. He was like a father to me and after his retirement he wrote to me every Christmas. I felt it deeply when he died, two years ago.'

The old man suddenly stopped speaking and his eyes shone with a suspicious moisture.

'Do you think I could photograph Colonel Hutchings on his tomb?' I asked.

The old Rissaldar thought for a moment and said 'Yes, I think it is possible. The best time would be at midnight. Two days hence the moon will be full; if the Sahib were to go to the cemetery then, he might catch the Colonel Sahib.'

'Splendid! You must come too. I shall drive you there.'

'Very well, I shall be happy to do anything that will give the Sahib pleasure.'

At 9 p.m. two days later, the old Rissaldar presented himself at my bungalow, ready for the drive to Sirur. As I was about to take the wheel, I noticed that he had no overcoat. It was March and the nights were still chilly and my car was an open one.

'You cannot drive without an overcoat, Rissaldar Sahib; you must take one of mine, otherwise you will catch your death of cold.' So saying I ordered my servant to fetch a discarded ulster. I wrapped it round the old warrior and gave him a spare muffler as well to keep his throat warm. He accepted them gratefully. Motorcars did not then move as fast as they do now and it was just on midnight when we reached the Sirur cemetery. We got out and looked at the graveyard from a distance. Seen by the full March moon, it was an awe-inspiring sight.

'Let me go alone, Sahib,' whispered the Rissaldar. 'Hutchings Sahib may not wish to shew himself to a stranger.'

I agreed and the Rissaldar entered the graveyard, while I, concealed among the shrubbery, waited outside. Acting on my instructions, he placed the Kodak on a tomb some thirty feet from the Colonel's monument, gave the film a long exposure and, dropping the shutter, rejoined me. We drove back to Poona and in the small hours parted excellent friends, the Rissaldar returning me my ulster and muffler. I told him to come back in a week's time so that we might examine together the developed proof. Seven days later, about 9 a.m., the peon announced the Rissaldar. A packet of proofs had arrived the day before, but I had not opened it. I wished to do so in the old man's presence. Among the proofs was that of the Sirur cemetery. I handed it to the Rissaldar without looking at it closely. He cast his eyes over it and exclaimed: 'There he is, the Colonel Sahib, there he is! And the widow woman is there, too. I saw them both in the cemetery.'

I took the proof from my friend's hands and, sure enough, there, seated on the plinth of the monument, was the shadowy form of an Englishman in old-fashioned dress.

'I see the Colonel Sahib; but where is his wife whom you

call the widow woman?'

'I call her the widow woman,' said the Rissaldar Major severely, 'because in our caste there is no widow remarriage and she had no right to marry again. Still I see her; she is there coming behind from another tombstone to join him.'

I looked where the old soldier pointed and there did seem to be something that might have been the late Mrs Hutchings. About the Colonel himself there could be no doubt whatever; and I still treasure the photograph of the graveyard, doubly strange because of its weird appearance by moonlight and the uncanny figure of the Englishman sitting on the plinth of the central monument.

I took out my note case and tried to induce the Rissaldar to accept a hundred rupees, but I was severely snubbed. He said with dignity, 'A Shinde of Kizarnagar does not accept money for doing an act of courtesy that any gentleman might do for another.'

BOOMERANG

Oscar Cook

Warwick threw himself into a chair beside me, hitched up his trousers, and, leaning across, tapped me on the knee. 'You remember the story about Mendingham which you told me?' he asked.

I nodded. I was not likely to forget that affair. 'Well,' he went on, 'I've got as good a one to tell you. Had it straight from the filly's mouth, so to speak—and it's red-hot.'

I edged away in my chair, for there was something positively ghoulish in his delight, in the coarse way by which he referred to a woman, and one who, if my inference were correct, must have known tragedy. But there is no stopping Warwick: he knows or admits no finer feelings or shame when his thirst for 'copy' is aroused. Like the little boy in the well-known picture, 'he won't be happy till he's "quenched" it'.

I ordered drinks, and when they had been served and we were alone, bade him get on with his sordid story.

'It's a wild tale,' he began, 'of two planter fellows in the interior of Borneo—and, as usual, there's a woman.'

'*The* woman?' I could not refrain from asking, thinking of his earlier remark.

'The same,' he replied. 'A veritable golden-haired filly, only her mane is streaked with grey and there's a great livid scar or weal right round her neck. She's the wife of Leopold Thring. The other end of the triangle is Clifford Macy.'

'And where do you come in?' I inquired.

Warwick closed one eye and pursed his lips.

'As a spinner of yarns,' he answered sententiously. Then, with a return to his usual cynicism, 'The filly is down and out, but for some silly religious scruples feels she must live. I bought the story, therefore, after verifying the facts. Shall I go on?'

I nodded, for I must admit I was genuinely interested. The eternal triangle always intrigues: set in the wilds of Borneo it promised a variation of incident unusually refreshing in these sophisticated days. Besides, that scar was eloquent.

Warwick chuckled.

'The two men were partners,' he went on, 'on a small experimental estate far up in the interior. They had been at it for six years and were just about to reap the fruits of their labours very handsomely. Incidentally, Macy had been out in the Colony the full six years—and the strain was beginning to tell. Thring had been home eighteen months before, and on coming back had brought his bride, Rhona.

'That was the beginning of the trouble. It split up the partnership; brought in a new element: meant the building of a new bungalow.'

'For Macy?' I asked.

'Yes. And he didn't take kindly to it. He had got set. And then there was the loneliness of night after night alone, while the others—you understand?'

I nodded.

'Well,' Warwick continued, 'the expected happened. Macy flirted, philandered, and then fell violently in love. He was one of those fellows who never did things by halves. If he drank, he'd get fighting drunk: if he loved, he went all out on it: if he hated—well, hell was let loose.'

'And—Mrs Thring?' I queried, for it seemed to me that she might have a point of view.

'Fell between two stools—as so many women of a certain type do. She began by being just friendly and kind—you know the sort of thing—cheering the lonely man up, drifted into woman's eternal game of flirting, and then began to grow a little afraid of the fire she'd kindled. Too late she realized that she couldn't put the fire out—either hers or Macy's—and all the while she clung to some hereditary religious scruples.

'Thring was in many ways easy-going, but at the same time possessed of a curiously intense strain of jealous possessiveness. He was generous, too. If asked, he would share or give away his last shirt or crust. But let him think or feel that his rights or dues were being curtailed or taken and—well, he was a tough customer of rather primitive ideas.

'Rhona—that's the easiest way to think of the filly—soon found she was playing a game beyond her powers. Hers was no poker face, and Thring began to sense that something was wrong. She couldn't dissemble, and Macy made no attempt to hide his feelings. He didn't make it easy for her, and I guess from what the girl told me, life about this time was for her a sort of glorified hell—a suspicious husband on one hand, and an impetuous, devil-may-care lover on the other. She was living on a volcano.'

'Which might explode any minute.' I quietly said.

Warwick nodded.

'Exactly; or whenever Thring chose to spring the mine. He held the key to the situation, or, should I say, the time-fuse?

The old story, but set in a primitive land full of possibilities. You've got me?'

For answer I offered Warwick a cigarette, and, taking one myself lighted both.

'So far,' I said, 'with all your journalistic skill you've not got off the beaten track. Can't you improve?'

He chuckled, blew a cloud of smoke, and once again tapped my knee in his irritating manner.

'Your cynicism,' he countered, 'is but a poor cloak for your curiosity. In reality you're jumping mad to know the end, eh?'

I made no reply, and he went on.

'Well, matters went on from day to day till Rhona became worn to the proverbial shadow. Thring wanted to send her home, but she wouldn't go. She owed a duty to her husband: she couldn't bear to be parted from her lover, and she didn't dare leave the two men alone. She was terribly, horribly afraid.

'Macy grew more and more openly amorous and less restrained. Thring watched whenever possible with the cunning of an iguana. Then came a rainy, damp spell that tried the nerves to the uttermost and the inevitable stupid little disagreements between Rhona and Thring—mere trifles, but enough to let the lid off. He challenged her—'

'And she?' I could not help asking, for Warwick has, I must admit, the knack of keeping one on edge.

'Like a blithering but sublime little idiot admitted that it was all true.'

For nearly a minute, I was speechless. Somehow, although underneath I had expected Rhona to behave so, it seemed such a senseless, unbelievable thing to do. Then at last I found my voice.

'And Thring?' I said simply.

Warwick emptied his glass at a gulp.

'That's the most curious thing in the whole yarn,' he answered slowly 'Thring took it as quietly as a lamb.'

'Stunned?' I suggested.

'That's what Rhona thought: what Macy believed when Rhona told him what had happened. In reality he must have been burning mad, a mass of white-hot revenge controlled by a devilish, cunning brain: he waited. A scene or a fight—and Macy was a big man—would have done no good. He would get his own back in his own time and in his own way. Meanwhile, there was the lull before the storm.

'Then, as so often happens, fate played a hand. Macy went sick with malaria—really ill—and even Thring had to admit the necessity for Rhona to nurse him practically night and day. Macy owned his eventual recovery to her care, but even so his convalescence was a long job. In the end Rhona, too, crocked up through overwork, and Thring had them both on his hands. This was an opportunity better than he could have planned—it separated the lovers and gave him complete control.

'Obviously the time was ripe, ripe for Thring to score his revenge. The rains were over, the jungle had ceased wintering, and spring was in the air. The young grass and vegetation were shooting into new life: concurrently all the creepy, crawly insect life of the jungle and estate was young and vigorous and hungry, too. These facts gave Thring the germ of an idea which he was not slow to perfect—an idea as devilish as man could devise.'

Warwick paused to press out the stub of his cigarette, and noticing that even he seemed affected by his recital, I prepared myself as best I could for a really gruesome horror. All I said however, was, 'Go on.'

'It seems,' he continued, 'that in Borneo there is a kind of mammoth earwig—a thing almost as fine and gossamer as a spider's web, as long as a good-sized caterpillar, that lives on waxy secretions. These are integral parts of some flowers and trees, and lie buried deep in their recesses. It is one of the terrors of these particular tropics, for it moves and rests so lightly on a human being that one is practically unconscious of it, while, like its English relation, it has a decided liking for the human ear: on account of man's carnivorous diet the wax in this has a strong and very succulent taste.'

As Warwick gave me those details, he sat upright on the edge of his easy-chair. He spoke slowly, emphasizing each point by hitting the palm of his left hand with the clenched first of his right. It was impossible not to see the drift and inference of his remarks.

'You mean?' I began.

'Exactly,' he broke in quickly, blowing a cloud of smoke from a fresh cigarette which he had nervously lighted. 'Exactly. It was a devilish idea. To put the giant earwig on Macy's hair just above the ear.'

'And then...?' I knew the fatuousness of the question, but speech relieved the growing sense of ticklish horror that was creeping over me.

'Do nothing. But rely on the filthy insect running true to type. Once in Macy's ear, it was a thousand-to-one chance against it ever coming out the same way: it would not be able to turn: to back out would be almost an impossibility, and so, feeding as it went, it would crawl right across inside his head, with the result that—'

The picture Warwick was drawing was more than I could bear: even my imagination, dulled by years of legal dry-as-dust affairs, saw and sickened at the possibilities. I put out a hand

and gripped Warwick's arm.

'Stop, man!' I cried hoarsely 'For god's sake, don't say any more. I understand. My god, but the man Thring must be a fiend!'

Warwick looked at me, and I saw that even his face had paled.

'*Was,*' he said meaningly. 'Perhaps you're right, perhaps he *was* a fiend. Yet, remember, Macy stole his wife.'

'But a torture like that! The deliberate creation of a living torment that would grow into madness. Warwick, you can't condone that!'

He looked at me for a moment and then slowly spread out his hands.

'Perhaps you're right,' he admitted. 'It was a bit thick, I know. But there's more to come.'

I closed my eyes and wondered if I could think of an excuse for leaving Warwick; but in spite of my real horror, my curiosity won the day.

'Get on with it,' I muttered, and leant back, eyes still shut hands clenched. With teeth gritted together as if I myself were actually suffering the pain of that earwig slowly, daily creeping farther into and eating my brain, I waited.

Warwick was not slow to obey.

'I have told you,' he said, 'that Rhona had to nurse Macy, and even when he was better, though still weak, Thring insisted on her looking after him, though now he himself came more often.

'One afternoon Rhona was in Macy's bungalow alone with him: the house-boy was out. Rhona was on the verandah; Macy was asleep in the bedroom. Dusk was just falling; bats were flying about: the flying foxes, heavy with fruit, were returning home; the inevitable house rats were scurrying about the floors; the lamps had not been lit. An eerie, devastating hour. Rhona dropped some needlework and fought back tears. Then from the bedroom came a shriek: "My head! My ear! Oh, god! My ear! Oh, god! The pain!"

'That was the beginning. The earwig had got well inside. Rhona rushed in and did all she could. Of course, there was nothing to see. Then for a little while Macy would be quiet because the earwig was quiet, sleeping or gorged. Then the vile tiling would move or feed again, and Macy once more would shriek with the pain.

'And so it went on, day by day. Alternate quiet and alternate pain, each day for Macy, for Rhona a hell of nerve-rending expectancy. Waiting, always waiting for the pain that crept and crawled and twisted and writhed and moved slowly, ever slowly, through and across Macy's brain.'

Warwick paused so long that I was compelled to open my eyes. His face was ghastly. Fortunately I could not see my own.

'And Thring?' I asked.

'Came often each day. Pretended sorrow and served out spurious dope—Rhona found the coloured water afterwards. He cleverly urged that Macy should be carried down to the coast for medical treatment, knowing full well that he was too ill and worn to bear the smallest strain. Then when Macy was an utter wreck, broken completely in mind and body, with hollow, hunted eyes, with ever-twitching fingers, with a body no part of which he could properly control or keep still, the earwig came out—at the other ear.

'As it happened, both Thring and Rhona were present. Macy must have suffered an excruciating pain, followed as usual by a period of quiescence: then, feeling a slight ticklish sensation on his cheek, put up his hand to rub or scratch. His fingers came in contact with the earwig and its fine gossamer hair. Instinct did the rest. You follow?'

My tongue was still too dry to enable me to speak. Instead I nodded, and Warwick went on.

'He naturally was curious and looked to see what he was holding. In an instant, he realized. Even Rhona could not be in doubt. The hair was faintly but unmistakably covered here and there with blood, with wax and with grey matter.

'For a moment there was absolute silence between the three. At last Macy spoke.

'"My god!" he just whispered. "Oh, my god! What an escape!"

'Rhona burst into tears. Only Thring kept silent, and that was his mistake. The silence worried Macy, weak though he was. He looked from Rhona to Thring, and at the critical moment Thring could not meet his gaze. The truth was out. With an oath Macy *threw* the insect, now dead from the pressure of his fingers, straight into Thring's face. Then he crumpled up in his chair and sobbed and sobbed till even the chair shook.'

Again Warwick paused till I thought he would never go on. I had heard enough, I'll admit, and yet it seemed to me that at least there should be an epilogue.

'Is that all?' I tentatively asked.

Warwick shook his head.

'Nearly, but not quite,' he said. 'Rhona had ceased weeping and kept her eyes fixed on Thring—she dared not go and comfort Macy now. She saw him examine the dead earwig, having picked it up from the floor to which it had fallen, turn it this way and that, then produce from a pocket a magnifying-glass which he used daily for the inspection and detection of leaf disease on certain of the plants. As she watched, she saw the fear and disappointment leave his face, to be replaced by a look of cunning and evil satisfaction. Then for the first time he spoke.

"'Macy!" he called, in a sharp, loud voice.

'Macy looked up.

'Thring held up the earwig. "This is dead now," he said, "dead. As dead as my friendship for you, you swine of a thief, as dead as my love for that whore who was my wife. It's dead, I tell you, dead, but it's a female. D'you get me? A female, and a female lays eggs, and before it died it—"

'He never finished. His baiting at last roused Macy, endowing him with the strength of madness and despair. With one spring, he was at Thring's throat, bearing him down to the ground. Over and over they rolled on the floor, struggling for the possession of the great hunting-knife stuck in Thring's belt. One moment, Macy was on top, the next, Thring. Their breath and oaths came in great trembling gasps. They kicked and bit and scratched. And all the while Rhona watched, fascinated and terrified. Then Thring got definitely on top. He had one hand on Macy's throat, both knees on his chest, and with his free hand he was feeling for the knife. In that instant Rhona's religious scruples went by the board. She realized she only loved Macy, that her husband didn't count. She rushed to Macy's help. Thring saw her coming and let drive a blow at her head which almost stunned her. She fell on top of him just as he was whipping out the knife. Its edge caught her neck. The sudden spurt of blood shot into Thring's eyes, and blinded him. It was Macy's last chance. He knew it, and he took it.

'When Rhona came back to consciousness, Thring was dead. Macy was standing beside the body, which was gradually swelling to huge proportions as he worked, weakly but steadily, at the white ant exterminator pump, the nozzle of which was pushed down the dead man's throat.'

Warwick ceased. This last had been a long, unbroken recital, and mechanically he picked up his empty glass as if to drain it. The action brought me back to nearly normal. I rang for the waiter—the knob of the electric bell luckily being just over my head. While waiting, I had time to speak.

'I've heard enough,' I said hurriedly, 'to last me a lifetime. You've made me feel positively sick. But there's just one point. What happened to Macy? Did he live?'

Warwick nodded.

'That's another strange fact. He still lives. He was tried for the murder of Thring, but there was no real evidence. On the other hand, his story was too tall to be believed, with the result—well, you can guess.'

'A lunatic asylum—for life?' I asked.

Warwick nodded again. Then I followed his glance. A waiter was standing by my chair.

'Two double whisky-and-sodas,' I ordered tersely, and then, with shaking fingers, lighted a cigarette.

SUSANNA'S SEVEN HUSBANDS

Ruskin Bond

Locally, the tomb was known as 'the grave of the seven-times married one'.

You'd be forgiven for thinking it was Bluebeard's grave; he was reputed to have killed several wives in turn because they showed undue curiosity about a locked room. But this was the tomb of Susanna Anna-Maria Yeates, and the inscription (most of it in Latin) stated that she was mourned by all who had benefited from her generosity, her beneficiaries having included various schools, orphanages, and the church across the road. There was no sign of any other graves in the vicinity, and presumably her husbands had been interred in the old Rajpur graveyard, below the Delhi Ridge.

I was still in my teens when I first saw the ruins of what had once been a spacious and handsome mansion. Desolate and silent, its well-laid paths were overgrown with weeds, its flower-beds had disappeared under a growth of thorny jungle. The two-storeyed house had looked across the Grand Trunk Road. Now abandoned, feared and shunned, it stood encircled in mystery, reputedly the home of evil spirits.

Outside the gate, along the Grand Trunk Road, thousands of vehicles sped by—cars, trucks, buses, tractors, bullock-carts—but few noticed the old mansion or its mausoleum, set back as they were from the main road, hidden by mango, neem and peepul trees. One old and massive peepul tree grew out of the ruins of the house, strangling it much as its owner was said to have strangled one of her dispensable paramours.

As a much-married person with a quaint habit of disposing of her husbands, whenever she tired of them, Susanna's malignant spirit was said to haunt the deserted garden. I had examined the tomb, I had gazed upon the ruins, I had scrambled through shrubbery and overgrown rose-bushes, but I had not encountered the spirit of this mysterious woman. Perhaps, at the time, I was too pure and innocent to be targeted by malignant spirits. For, malignant she must have been, if the stories about her were true.

No one had been down into the vaults of the ruined mansion. They were said to be occupied by a family of cobras, traditional guardians of buried treasure. Had she really been a woman of great wealth, and could treasure still be buried there? I put these questions to Naushad, the furniture-maker, who had lived in the vicinity all his life, and whose father had made the furniture and fittings for this and other great houses in Old Delhi.

'Lady Susanna, as she was known, was much sought after for her wealth,'recalled Naushad. She was no miser, either. She spent freely, reigning in state in her palatial home, with many horses and carriages at her disposal. You see the stables there, behind the ruins? Now, they are occupied by bats and jackals. Every evening she rode through the Roshanara Gardens, the cynosure of all eyes, for she was beautiful as well as wealthy. Yes, all men sought her favours, and she could choose from the best of them. Many were fortune-hunters. She did not discourage them. Some found favour for a time, but she soon tired of them. None of her husbands enjoyed her wealth for very long!

'Today, no one enters those ruins, where once there was mirth and laughter. She was the zamindari lady, the owner of much land, and she administered her estate with a strong hand. She was kind if rents were paid when they fell due, but terrible if someone failed to pay.'

'Well, over fifty years have gone by since she was laid to rest, but still men speak of her with awe. Her spirit is restless, and it is said that she often visits the scenes of her former splendour. She has been seen walking through this gate, or riding in the gardens, or driving in her phaeton down the Rajpur road.'

'And, what happened to all those husbands?' I asked.

'Most of them died mysterious deaths. Even the doctors were baffled. Tomkins Sahib drank too much. The lady soon tired of him. A drunken husband is a burdensome creature, she was heard to say. He would have drunk himself to death, but she was an impatient woman and was anxious to replace him. You see those datura bushes growing wild in the grounds? They have always done well here.'

'Belladonna?' I suggested.

'That's right, huzoor. Introduced in the whisky-soda, they put him to sleep for ever.'

'She was quite humane in her way.'

'Oh, very humane, sir. She hated to see anyone suffer. One sahib, I don't know his name, drowned in the tank behind the house, where the water-lilies grew. But she made sure he was half-dead before he fell in. She had large, powerful hands, they said.'

'Why did she bother to marry them? Couldn't she just have had men friends?'

'Not in those days, dear sir. Respectable society would not have tolerated it. Neither in India nor in the West would it have been permitted.'

'She was born out of her time,' I remarked.

'True, sir. And remember, most of them were fortune-hunters. So, we need not waste too much pity on them.'

'*She* did not waste any.'

'She was without pity. Especially when she found out what they were really after. The snakes had a better chance of survival.'

'How did the other husbands take their leave of this world?'

'Well, the Colonel-sahib shot himself while cleaning his rifle. Purely an accident, huzoor. Although some say she had loaded his gun without his knowledge. Such was her reputation by now that she was suspected even when innocent. But she bought her way out of trouble. It was easy enough, if you were wealthy.'

'And, the fourth husband?'

'Oh, he died a natural death. There was a cholera epidemic that year, and he was carried off by the haija. Although, again, there were some who said that a good dose of arsenic produced the same symptoms! Anyway, it was cholera on the death certificate. And, the doctor who signed it was the next to marry her.'

'Being a doctor, he was probably quite careful about what he ate and drank.

'He lasted about a year.'

'What happened?'

'He was bitten by a cobra.'

'Well, that was just bad luck, wasn't it? You could hardly blame it on Susanna.'

'No, huzoor, but the cobra was in his bedroom. It was coiled around the bed-post. And, when he undressed for the night, it struck! He was dead when Susanna came into the room an hour later. She had a way with snakes. She did not harm them and they never attacked her.'

'And, there were no antidotes in those days. Exit the doctor. Who was the sixth husband?'

'A handsome man. An indigo planter. He had gone bankrupt when the indigo trade came to an end. He was hoping to recover his fortune with the good lady's help. But our Susanna-mem, she did not believe in sharing her fortune with anyone.'

'How did she remove the indigo planter?'

'It was said that she lavished strong drink upon him, and when he lay helpless, she assisted him on the road we all have to take by pouring molten lead in his ears.'

'A painless death, I'm told.'

'But a terrible price to pay huzoor, simply because one is no longer needed...'

We walked along the dusty highway, enjoying the evening breeze, and some time later we entered the Roshanara Gardens, in those days Delhi's most popular and fashionable meeting place.

'You have told me how six of her husbands died, Naushad. I thought there were seven?'

'Ah, a gallant young magistrate, who perished right here, huzoor. They were driving through the park after dark when the lady's carriage was attacked by brigands. In defending her, the gallant young man received a fatal sword wound.'

'Not the lady's fault, Naushad.'

'No, my friend. But he was a magistrate, remember, and the assailants, one of whose relatives had been convicted by him, were out for revenge. Oddly enough, though, two of the men were given employment by the lady Susanna at a later date. You may draw your own conclusions.'

'And, were there others?'

'Not husbands. But an adventurer, a soldier of fortune came along. He found her treasure, they say. He lies buried with it, in the cellars of the ruined house. His bones lie scattered there, among gold and silver and precious jewels. The cobras guard them still! But how he perished was a mystery, and remains so till this day.'

'What happened to Susanna?'

'She lived to a good old age, as you know. If she paid for her crimes, it wasn't in this life! As you know, she had no children. But she started an orphanage and gave generously to the poor and to various schools and institutions, including a home for widows. She died peacefully in her sleep.'

'A merry widow,' I remarked. 'The Black Widow spider!'

Don't go looking for Susanna's tomb. It vanished some years ago, along with the ruins of her mansion. A smart new housing estate came up on the site, but not after several workmen and a contractor succumbed to snake bite! Occasionally, residents complain of a malignant ghost in their midst, who is given to flagging down cars, especially those driven by single men. There have been one or two mysterious disappearances. Ask anyone living along this stretch of the Delhi Ridge, and they'll tell you that's it's true.

And, after dusk, an old-fashioned horse and carriage can sometimes be seen driving through the Roshanara Gardens. Ignore it, my friend. Don't stop to answer any questions from the beautiful fair lady who smiles at you from behind lace curtains. She's still looking for a suitable husband.